"James Bravo, you may kiss your bride."

Addie was looking up
eyes, already feeling t
jackpot as far as tempo

And then James slowly
realized that it was actually happening: they were
about to share their first kiss.

James said her name softly, in that wonderful
smooth, deep voice of his that sent little thrills of
excitement pulsing all through her.

She said, "James," low and sweet, just for him. And
she thought of the last three nights, of the two of
them together in the hotel room bed. Of waking up
each morning cuddled up close to him, of one of
the other of them gently reluctantly pulling away...

Okay, maybe it wasn't a *real* marriage. And it would
be over as soon as her grandfather was back on his
feet.

So what? It was probably as close to a real marriage
as she was ever going to get.

* * *

THE BRAVOS OF JUSTICE CREEK:
Where bold hearts collide under Western skies

Dear Reader

Every once in a while I just have to kick over the traces and write a rollicking, wild and woolly modern-day Western romance. *James Bravo's Shotgun Bride* is one of those.

Addie Kenwright is pregnant. Her dear old grandpa Levi is absolutely certain that James Bravo must be the dad. Levi's seen Addie and James together, and Addie may be pretending that nothing's going on with James, but Levi knows undeniable mutual attraction when he sees it.

So Levi decides to take matters into his own hands. He knows where to find James and he knows how to convince that hardheaded Bravo man to do the right thing, because Levi's coming grandbaby deserves both a mommy *and* a daddy.

Everything is going to work out as it should. With the help of his pump-action Mossburg Maverick 88, Levi intends to make everything right.

Happy reading everyone,

Christine Rimmer

James Bravo's Shotgun Bride

Christine Rimmer

Recycling programs
for this product may
not exist in your area

978-0-373-65956-2

James Bravo's Shotgun Bride

Printed in U.S.A.

Christine Rimmer came to her profession the long way around. She tried everything from acting to teaching to telephone sales. Now she's finally found work that suits her perfectly. She insists she never had a problem keeping a job—she was merely gaining "life experience" for her future as a novelist. Christine lives with her family in Oregon. Visit her at christinerimmer.com.

Books by Christine Rimmer

Harlequin Special Edition

The Bravos of Justice Creek

Carter Bravo's Christmas Bride
The Good Girl's Second Chance
Not Quite Married

The Bravo Royales

A Bravo Christmas Wedding
The Earl's Pregnant Bride
The Prince's Cinderella Bride
Holiday Royale
How to Marry a Princess
Her Highness and the Bodyguard
The Rancher's Christmas Princess

Bravo Family Ties

A Bravo Homecoming
Marriage, Bravo Style!
Donovan's Child
Expecting the Boss's Baby

Montana Mavericks: What Happened at the Wedding?

The Maverick's Accidental Bride

Montana Mavericks: 20 Years in the Saddle!

Million-Dollar Maverick

Montana Mavericks: Rust Creek Cowboys

Marooned with the Maverick

Montana Mavericks: The Texans are Coming!

The Last Single Maverick

Visit the Author Profile page at Harlequin.com for more titles.

For Anita Hayes,
crafter, great cook
and world's most attentive raiser of chickens.
You make me laugh and touch my heart.
This one's for you, Anitabug.

Chapter One

Waking up tied to a chair is bad.

But waking up tied to a chair staring down the deadly single barrel of old Levi Kenwright's pump-action shotgun?

So. Much. Worse.

James Bravo stifled a groan. Not only did it appear he was about to eat serious lead, but he had the mother of all headaches. Surely Levi didn't really intend to shoot him. James shook his head, hoping to clear it.

Still a little fuzzy. And still hurt, too. And Levi still had that shotgun trained right on him.

The old man wasn't at his best. His wiry white hair looked as if he'd combed it with a cattle prod and his craggy face seemed kind of pale—except for two spots of color, burning red, cresting his cheekbones. Sweat shone on his wrinkled throat and darkened the underarms of his worn checked shirt.

His aim, however?

Way too steady. Levi grunted as he sighted down the barrel. "Good. You're awake. I was beginnin' to worry I'd hit you a mite hard."

James winced, blinked in another failed attempt to ease his pounding head and cast a careful glance around him. Judging by the lack of windows, the knotty pine paneling, the faint smell of cool earth and the stairs leading upward along the far wall, Levi had brought him to a basement. Was it the basement of the house at Red Hill Ranch, where Levi lived with his way too damn attractive granddaughter Addie?

Probably.

On the battered pasteboard side table a few feet away, James spotted his phone, his wallet and his keys. So even if he managed to get his hand into his pocket, there was no phone in there to use to call for help.

And just how in hell had all of this happened?

James remembered standing on the porch of his nearly finished new house ten miles outside his hometown of Justice Creek, Colorado. It was a cool and sunny March afternoon. He'd been gazing off toward the big weathered barn at Red Hill, hoping that Addie would soon ride by on one of those horses she boarded and trained.

The crazy old coot must have come up on him from behind.

Cautiously, James inquired, "Er, Mr. Kenwright?"

"No need for formalities, son," Levi replied downright pleasantly as he continued to point the shotgun at James. "We're gonna be family. I want you to call me Levi."

Had the old man just said they were going to be… family? James's head hurt too much for him to even try to get a handle on that one. "Levi it is, then."

A wry little chortle escaped the wild-haired old man. "That's better."

Better? Better would be if Levi put down the gun and untied him immediately. But James didn't say that. For the time being, he would say nothing that might rile his captor. A riled Levi could suddenly decide to fire that shotgun. That would be good and bad. Good, because James would no longer have a headache. Bad, because he wouldn't have a head, either.

"Levi, do you mind if I ask you something?"

"You go right ahead, son."

"Why am I tied to a chair in the basement of your house?"

Another chortle. And then, very slowly, Levi lowered the shotgun. James drew a cautious breath of relief as Levi replied, "Good question. And one I am sure you will know the answer to if you just give it a little more thought."

James closed his eyes. He thought. But thinking gave him nothing, except to make his head pound harder. "Sorry, but I honestly have no idea why you're doing this to me."

"Well, then." Levi backed three steps, sank into the battered leather easy chair behind him and laid the shotgun across his knees. "Allow me to explain."

"Wonderful. Thank you."

"Think nothin' of it—I know you know my granddaughter Addison."

"Of course I know Addie." Was she somehow involved in this? Why? He'd done nothing to cause her to make her grandfather hit him on the head, drag him to Red Hill and tie him to a chair.

Had he?

"Means everything to me, that girl," Levi said. "She

and her big sister, Carmen, are what I got that matters in this world—well, them and my great-grandkids, Tammy and Ian, and their dad, Devin. A fine lad, Devin. Like you, he needed a little convincing. But once he understood the situation, he stepped right up. Same as you're gonna do—and where was I?"

"Uh, Addie and the rest of your family mean everything to you?"

"Right. Family, son. Family is everything. So you can imagine my concern when I recently discovered that Addie's in the *family* way." *Addie pregnant? Could that be true?* Levi went right on. "Naturally, I want my new great-grandbaby to have two parents. That's the old-fashioned way, which is to say, it is God's way. And that means it's the *best* way. And of course, I know very well that *you* are my new great-grandbaby's daddy. So I'm just helping things along a little here, just nudging you down the path known as doing the right thing."

James cleared his throat. Carefully. "Hold on a minute…"

"Yeah?"

James had a strong suspicion that there was a lump on the back of his head where Levi had hit him. The lump throbbed. It felt like a big lump, a lump that was growing bigger as he tried to make sense of what Addie's crazy grandpa said to him. "Did you just say that Addie's having my baby?"

Holding the shotgun between his two gnarled fists, looking weary as a traveler at the end of a very long road, Levi rose to his feet again. "Your baby needs a daddy, son. And my Addie needs a husband." He raised the gun and aimed the damn thing at James's aching head once more. "So tell me, is the path becoming clearer now?"

James had never had sex with Addie. Never kissed her, never done more than brush a touch against her hand.

True, he would very much have liked to do any number of things to Addie. But he hadn't. So if Addie had a little one on the way, he wasn't the man responsible.

And that he wasn't really pissed him off.

But James's jealousy of some mystery man who got a whole lot luckier than he ever had was not the issue here.

The issue was that Levi had kidnapped the wrong guy.

Not that James had any intention of setting the old codger straight. Not at the moment, anyway. James had more sense than to argue with a man who'd already cold-cocked him, abducted him and tied him to a chair.

Yeah. Levi meant business, all right. And it was looking more and more likely that the old guy had a screw loose. James was a lawyer by profession. He'd dealt with more than one screwball client in his career. Arguing with a nutcase had never gotten him anywhere.

So instead of insisting he'd never laid a hand on Addie, James announced with all the sincerity he could muster, "Levi, the right thing is exactly what I want to do."

"Glad to hear it, son."

"Great, then. If you'll just untie—"

"Not. Quite. Yet." Levi shook his head, but at least he lowered the gun again.

Keeping it cool, James breathed slowly and carefully. "All righty, Levi. When, exactly, *do* you plan to untie me?"

"Soon as I'm absolutely certain you're not gonna pull any tricks on me. Soon as I know I can count on you to…" Levi's sentence died unfinished as a door slammed shut upstairs. The old man gasped. His rheumy eyes widened as footsteps echoed from above.

Addie. James's heart leaped as his head pounded harder. Had to be Addie.

And it was. "PawPaw!" she hollered, the sound far

away, muffled, not coming from whatever room was directly overhead. "Where are you?"

James and Levi both stared at the ceiling, tracking the path of her quick, firm footsteps on the floor above as those footsteps came closer.

And closer…

They passed right overhead.

The basement door squeaked as it opened. James couldn't see that door, not from where he was tied in the middle of the basement floor. But he heard Addie crystal clear now as she called down the stairs, "PawPaw?"

"Don't you come down here!" Levi glared at James and waved the shotgun threateningly for silence. "I'll be up in a minute!"

The door only creaked wider, followed by more creaking: footsteps on the stairs. A pair of tan boots appeared, descending, bringing with them shapely legs in a snug pair of faded jeans. "What are you up to down here?" The curvy top half of Addie came into view, including those beautiful breasts of hers in a tight T-shirt and all that softly curling ginger hair. About then, she turned and caught sight of James. Big golden-brown eyes went wide in surprise. "What the…?" She stumbled. A frantic screech escaped her as her booted feet flew out. She windmilled her arms.

"Addie!" James and Levi shouted their useless warnings simultaneously.

But then, with another cry, she grabbed the iron stair rail and righted herself just in time to keep from tumbling the rest of the way to the concrete floor.

"Get hold of yourself, girl," old Levi grumbled as she made it down the last step and sagged against the railing. "A woman in your condition has got to be careful."

Those baby-doll lips of hers flattened in a scowl and

two bright spots of color flared high on her round cheeks as she put a hand to her stomach and tried to catch her breath. "PawPaw, you're scaring me to death. Put down that gun and untie James immediately."

Levi lowered the gun, but he didn't put it down. "Now, Addie honey." His tone had turned coaxing. "I can't untie him right yet. First, James and I need to come to a clear understanding."

"An understanding of what?" Addie drew herself up, stuck out her pretty, round chin and glared daggers at Levi, who stared back at her sheepishly but didn't answer. He must have known she would figure it out—and she did. Her eyes went wide again as she put it together. "Have you lost your mind? I told you. James is not the guy."

Levi granted her a patient, disbelieving look—and explained to James, "Morning sickness. That's how I knew. Just like her grandma, her mom and her big sister, too. Morning sickness early and often. Then I found that little stick she used to take the test. I put it all together, yes, I did. Levi Kenwright is no fool."

Addie made a growling sound. She actually seemed to vibrate with frustration. "You had no right, PawPaw, none, to go snooping through my bathroom wastebasket. I told you what I think of that. That is just wrong. And now to *kidnap* poor James, too? What is the *matter* with you?"

"Nothing is the matter with me," Levi huffed. "I'm fixing things for you and James here, just like I fixed them for Carmen and Devin."

James decided he couldn't be hearing this right. Surely Levi wasn't implying that he'd kidnapped Carmen's husband, too?

Addie shrieked again, this time in fury. Waving her arms as she went, she started pacing back and forth across the big rag rug that anchored the makeshift basement living area. "How can I *talk* to you? You are impossible. You know very well that it was *wrong* of you to kidnap Devin."

Levi just stood there, cradling his shotgun, looking smug. "Worked, didn't it? Eight years later, he and Carmen and the kids are just as happy as bugs in a basket."

Addie stopped stock-still beside the ancient portable TV on its rickety stand. She sucked air like a bull about to charge. "I can't *talk* to you. I want to *kill* you." She planted her fists on her hips and commanded, "Untie James right this minute."

Levi didn't budge. "Now, Addie honey, don't get yourself all worked up. James has told me the truth, accepted his responsibility to you and the baby and promised to do the right thing."

Addie gasped in outrage and whipped her head around to glare at James. "You told him *what*?"

Oh, great. As if all this was his fault? He suggested mildly, "Given the situation, arguing with your grandfather didn't seem like a good idea."

"I don't… I can't…" Addie sputtered, furious, glancing back and forth between him and the old man. And then she pinned her grandfather with another baleful glare. "Of course James *confessed*. What choice did he have? You held a shotgun to his head."

Levi blustered, "He confessed because it's true and we both know that it is."

"No. No, it is *not* true. James is not my baby's daddy. How many ways can I say it? How in the hell am I going to get through to you?"

Levi made a humphing sound and flung out an arm in James's direction. "If not him, then who?"

By then, Addie's plump cheeks were beet red with

fury and frustration. She drew in a slow, hard breath. "Fine. All right. It is none of your business until I'm ready to tell you and you ought to know that. But if you just *have* to know, it's Brandon. Brandon is my baby's father."

Levi blinked three times in rapid succession. And then he let out a mocking cackle of a laugh. "Brandon Hall?"

James fully understood Levi's disbelief. A local poor boy made good who'd designed supersuccessful video games for a living, Brandon Hall was never all that hale and hearty. Recently, he'd died of cancer, having been bedridden for months before he passed on. It seemed pretty unlikely that Brandon had been in any condition to father a child—not in the last few months, anyway. And Addie's stomach was still flat. She couldn't be that far along. Uh-uh. James didn't buy Addie's story any more than Levi did.

"Yes," Addie insisted tightly. "Brandon *is* the dad."

"I may be old, but I'm not senile," Levi reminded her. "There is no way that Brandon Hall could've done what needed doing to put you in this predicament, Addison Anne, and you know that as well as I do."

Addie fumed some more. "You are so thickheaded. Honestly, I cannot talk to you…" She turned to James and spoke softly, gently. Soothingly, even. "I am so sorry, James, for what my grandpa has done." She gave him the big eyes. God, she was cute. "Are you hurt?"

He nodded, wincing. "He got the jump on me, whacked me on the back of the head, hard, out at my new place. Knocked me out cold. I'm not sure how long I was unconscious, but when I woke up, I was here."

She hissed in a breath and whirled to pin her grandfather with another accusing glare.

Levi played it off. "He's fine. Hardheaded. All the Bravos are. Everybody knows that."

"You *hit* him, Grandpa." She threw out a hand in James's direction. "You *hurt* him. And you have restrained him against his will." Levi started to speak. "Shush," she commanded. "Do not say another word to me. I can't even look at you right now." She turned back to James. "I really am so, so sorry…" James sat very still and tried his best to look appropriately noble and wounded. She came closer. "Can I…take a peek, see how bad it is?"

"Sure." He turned his head so she could see.

And then she was right there, bending over him, smelling of sunshine and clean hay and something else, something purely womanly, wonderfully sweet. "Oh!" she cried. "It's a big bump. And you're *bleeding…*"

"I'm all right," he said. It was the truth. The pain and the pounding had lessened in the past few minutes. And the closer Addie got, the better he felt. "And there's not *that* much blood—is there?"

"No, just a dribble of it. But blood is blood and that's not good."

He turned and met her enormous eyes. "I'll be all right. I'm sure I will."

She drew back. He wished she wouldn't. It was harder to smell her now she'd moved away. "I don't know what to say, James. I feel horrible about this. We need to patch you up immediately…"

"Don't untie him!" shouted Levi.

Addie just waved a hand in the old guy's direction and kept those big eyes on James. "Of course I will untie you."

"No!" Levi hollered.

She ignored him and spoke directly to James. "I will

untie you right now if you'll only promise me not to call the police on my crazy old granddad."

"I'm not crazy!" Levi huffed. "I'm not crazy and he's the dad—and you are not, under any circumstances, to untie him yet."

"Grandpa, he is *not* the dad. Brandon's the dad."

"No."

"Yeah—and if you just *have* to have all the gory details, Brandon was my lifelong friend." She choked a little then, emotion welling.

Levi only groaned in impatient disgust. "I know he was your friend. I also know that's *all* he was to you— nothing like you and lover boy here. Come on, Addie honey. I wasn't born yesterday. I've seen the way this man looks at you, the way he's been chasin' after you— and though I know you've been trying to pretend nothing's going on, it's plain as the nose on my face that you are just as gone on him as he is on you."

"She is?" James barely kept himself from grinning like a fool.

But no one was looking at him anyway. Levi kept arguing, "James is the daddy, no doubt about it. And, Addie girl, you need to quit telling your old PawPaw lies and admit the truth so that we can move on and fix what doesn't need to be broken."

"I am not lying," she cried. "Brandon was my best friend in the whole world and he grew up in foster care, with no family, with nothing."

"Stop tellin' me things I already know."

"What I am telling you is that he wanted a child, someone to carry on a little piece of him when he was gone. Before he got too sick, he took steps. He had his sperm frozen…" Addie sniffed. Her big eyes brimmed. She blinked furiously, but it was no good. She couldn't hold back her tears. They overflowed and ran down her cheeks. "And then he asked me if just maybe I would do that for him, if I would have his child so that something would be left of him in this world when he was nothing but ashes scattered on the cold ground…"

By then James was so caught up in the story he'd pretty much forgotten his own predicament. Everyone in Justice Creek knew that Addie Kenwright and Brandon Hall had been best friends from childhood. People said that, near the end, she'd spent every spare moment at Brandon's bedside. As the dead man had no one else, Addie had been the one to arrange the funeral service. She and Levi and her sister, Carmen, and Carmen's husband, Devin, had sat together in the front pew, all the family that Brandon had.

James asked her gently, "So, then, it was artificial insemination?"

Addie sniffed, swiped the tears with the back of her hand and nodded. "We tried three times. What's that they say? The third time's the charm? Well, it was. But Brandon died the day after the third time. He died not even knowing that he was going to be a dad."

James realized he was in awe of Addie Kenwright and her willingness to have a baby for her dying friend.

Levi, however, refused to accept that he'd kidnapped the wrong man. "That's the most ridiculous bunch of bull I've ever heard. And I'm seventy-eight years old, Addie Anne, so you'd better believe I've heard some tall tales in my lifetime."

Addie only swiped more tears away and moved to stand behind James again. He glanced over his shoulder at her. She met his eyes and said softly, "I just hope you'll be kind, that you'll take pity on an old man who never meant to hurt anyone."

"I will," he vowed quietly. "I do."

"Thank you." Her cool hands swift and capable, she began working at the knots Levi had used to bind him.

Levi let out another shout. "No!" He started waving the shotgun again. "Don't you do that, Addie Anne. Don't you dare. Under no circumstances can James be untied until I am absolutely certain that he's ready to do the right thing!"

Addie said nothing. She kept working the knots as Levi kept shouting, "Stop! Stop this instant!" He ran in circles, the gun held high.

Just as the ropes binding James went slack, Levi let out a strange, strangled cry. He clapped his hand to his chest—and let go of the shotgun.

The gun hit the floor. An ungodly explosion followed and a foot-wide hole bloomed in the ceiling. Addie screamed. Ears ringing, James jumped from the chair. Sheetrock, wood framing and kitchen flooring rained down.

And Levi, his face gone a scary shade of purple, keeled over on his back gasping and moaning, clutching his chest in a desperate, gnarled fist.

"PawPaw!" Addie cried and ran to him. She dropped to her knees at his side.

Levi gasped and groaned and clutched his chest even harder. "Shouldn't've…untied him…"

"Oh, dear God." She cast a quick, frantic glance in James's direction. "Call an ambulance. Please…"

James grabbed his phone off the side table and called 911.

Chapter Two

Once he got help on the line, James gave his phone to Addie so she could talk to the dispatcher directly. He scooped up his keys and wallet and stuck them in his pocket. And then he waited, ready to help in any way he might be needed.

Addie pulled his phone away from her ear. "You can go."

He didn't budge. "Later. What can I do?"

She listened on the phone again as Levi lay there groaning. "Yes," she said. "All right, yes." She made soothing sounds at Levi. Then she looked at James again. "If you could maybe go up and get a pillow from his bed. His room's off the front entry on the main floor. And get the aspirin from the medicine cabinet in the bathroom there?"

He was already on his way up the stairs. He found the pillow and the aspirin and ran them back down to her.

"Thank you," she said. "And really. We're okay. You just go ahead and go."

Levi was clearly very far from okay. James pretended he hadn't heard her and eased the pillow under Levi's head.

Addie gave the old man an aspirin. "Put it under your tongue and let it dissolve there." Levi grumbled out a few curse words, but he did what Addie told him to do. Addie shot another glance at James. "I mean it. Go on and get out of here."

Again, he ignored her. Not that he blamed her for wanting him to go, after all that had happened. But no way was he leaving her alone right now. What if Levi didn't make it? James would never forgive himself for running off and deserting them at a time like this, with Addie scared to death and Levi just lying there, sweating and moaning and clutching his chest as he tried to answer the questions that Addie relayed to him from the dispatcher.

At the last minute, as the ambulance siren wailed in the yard, James glanced up at the hole in the ceiling. He looked down at the rope abandoned on the rug at the base of the chair and the shotgun that had landed in front of the TV. All that was going to look pretty strange.

He couldn't do much about the hole, but he did grab the shotgun. He ejected the remaining shells and gathered them up, including the spent casing, which he found right out in the open in front of the sofa. He put the gun and the shells in the closet under the stairs and tossed the rope in there, too. The straight chair, he moved to a spot against the wall.

"Thank you," Addie said. He glanced over and saw she was watching him.

He shrugged. "There's still the hole in the ceiling. But don't worry. It'll be fine."

"Hope so."

"Just a little accident, that's all."

She pressed those fine lips together, her eyes full of fear for her grandpa. "Would you go up and show them down here?"

"You bet." He ran up the stairs and greeted the med techs. "Roberta," he said. "Sal." They were local people and he'd known them all his life.

Sal asked, "Where is he?"

"In the basement. This way…"

Roberta and Sal were pros. In no time, they had Levi on a stretcher, an oxygen mask on his face and an IV in his arm. James helped them get Levi up the stairs. As they put him in the ambulance, Addie ran back inside to grab her purse and lock up. Her sweet-natured chocolate Labrador retriever, Moose, followed after her, whining with concern. Addie told the dog to stay. With another worried whine, Moose trotted to the porch and dropped to his haunches. Addie climbed in the back of the ambulance with her grandfather and Roberta.

Sal went around and got in behind the wheel. James trailed after him.

"Who blew the hole in the kitchen floor?" Sal asked out the open driver's window as he started the engine.

"Levi was cleaning his shotgun."

Sal just shook his head. "You've got blood on your collar."

"It's nothing. You taking him to Justice Creek General?"

With a nod, Sal put it in gear.

A moment later, James stood there alone in the dirt yard a few feet from Levi's pre-WWII green Ford pickup, which had no doubt been used to kidnap him. Overhead, the sun beamed down. Not a cloud in the sky. It wasn't at all the kind of day a man expected to be kidnapped on.

Gently, he probed the goose egg on the back of his head. It was going to be fine. *He* was going to be fine.

Levi, though?

Hard to say.

And what about Addie, all on her own at Justice Creek General, waiting to hear if her granddad would make it or not? At a time like this, a woman should have family around her. Her half sister, Carmen, would come from Wyoming. But how long would it take for Carmen to arrive?

He just didn't like to think of Addie sitting in a hospital waiting room all alone.

As the ambulance disappeared around the first turn in the long driveway that led to the road, James took off toward the barn.

A couple of the horses Addie boarded watched him with mild interest as he jumped the fence into the horse pasture and ran until he got to the fence on the far side. He jumped that, too, and kept on running. Fifteen minutes after leaving Addie's front yard, he reached his quad cab, which was parked in front of his nearly finished new house. He had a bad cramp in his side and he had to walk in circles catching his breath, now and then bending over, sucking in air like a drowning man.

There was blood on his tan boots—not much, just a few drops. He pictured old Levi, hitting him on the head and then dragging him to that green Ford truck of his—and not only to the truck, but then out of the truck, into the house at Red Hill and down to the basement. No wonder the old fool had a heart attack.

As soon as his breath evened out a little, James dug his keys from his pocket and got in his quad cab. He checked his shirt collar in the sunscreen mirror. The blood wasn't that bad and the bump hardly hurt at all anymore.

He started the pickup and peeled out of there.

* * *

Addie needed to throw up. She needed to do that way too much lately. Right now, however, was not a convenient time. She sat in the molded plastic chair in the ER waiting room and pressed her hands over her mouth as she resolutely willed the contents of her stomach to stay down.

She had James's phone in her purse. In her frantic scramble to get in the ambulance with Levi, she hadn't thought to give the phone back. And then she'd clutched it like a lifeline all the way to the hospital. She'd only stuck it in her purse to free her hands when the reception clerk had given her all those forms to fill out.

Addie sucked in a slow breath and let it out even slower. *Oh, dear Lord, please. Let PawPaw pull through this and let me not throw up now.* Everything had happened way too fast. Her mind—and her poor stomach—was still struggling to catch up.

Her own cell phone was in her purse, too. She'd barely remembered to grab it off the front hall table before racing out the door. She needed to get it out and call Carmen in Laramie. But the nurse had said Levi wouldn't be in the ER for long. They would evaluate his condition and move him over to cardiac care for the next step. Addie was kind of waiting to find out what, exactly, the next step might be so that she could share it with her sister when she broke the terrifying news.

A door opened across the room. The doctor she'd talked to earlier emerged and came toward her.

Addie jumped to her feet, swallowed hard to keep from vomiting all over her boots and demanded, "My grandfather. Is he…?" Somehow she couldn't quite make herself ask the whole dangerous question.

"He's all right for now." The doctor, a tall, thin woman

with straight brown hair, spoke to her soothingly. "We've done a series of X-rays and given him medications to stabilize him."

"Stabilize him," Addie repeated idiotically. "Is that good? That's good, right?"

"Yes. But his X-rays show that he's got more than one artery blocked. He's going to need emergency open-heart surgery. We want to airlift him to Denver, to St. Anne's Memorial. It's a Level-One trauma center and they will be fully equipped to give him the specialized care that he needs."

Her head spun. Denver. Open-heart surgery. How could this be happening? From the moment she'd caught sight of James Bravo tied to a chair in the basement at Red Hill, nothing had seemed real. "But…he's never been sick a day in his life."

The doctor spoke gently, "It happens like this sometimes. That's why they call heart disease the silent killer. Too often, you only know you've got a problem when you have a heart attack—but I promise we're doing everything we can to get him the best care there is. You got him here quickly and that's a large part of the battle. His chances are good."

Good. His chances were good. Was the doctor just saying that or was it really true? Addie sucked in air slowly and ordered her queasy stomach to settle down. "Can I see my grandfather, please?"

"Of course you can. This way."

In the curtained-off cubicle, Addie kissed Levi's pale, wrinkled cheek and smoothed his wiry white hair and whispered, as much to reassure herself as to comfort him,

"PawPaw, I promise you, everything is going to be fine. You'll be on the mend before you know it."

Levi only groaned and demanded in a rough whisper, "Where's James?"

That made her long to start yelling at him again. But he looked so small and shrunken lying there, hooked up to an IV and a bunch of machines that monitored every breath he took, every beat of his overstressed heart. Yelling at him would have to wait until he was better.

Because he *would* get better. He *had* to get better. The alternative was simply unthinkable.

Right now nothing could be allowed to upset him. So she lied through her teeth. "James is out in front waiting to hear how you're doing."

"Good." Levi barely mouthed the word. "Good…" And then, with a long, tired sigh, he shut his eyes.

Addie bent close to him. "I love you, PawPaw." She kissed him and had to close her mind against the flood of tender images. Her mom had died having her and she'd never known her dad. All her memories of growing up, he was there for her, and for Carmen. He was their mom and their dad, all rolled into one cantankerous, dependable, annoyingly lovable package.

She could not—*would* not—lose him now.

A nurse pushed back the curtain and announced, "The critical-care helicopter has arrived. We need to get your grandfather on his way now."

"Can I ride with him?"

The nurse explained gently that there just wasn't room.

About then, Addie realized her pickup was back at the ranch. She'd have to call someone to give her a ride home so she could get herself to Denver. And what about the horses? She had to find someone to look after them at least until tomorrow. And she still really needed to call Carmen immediately.

She thanked the nurse, kissed her grandpa one more time and hustled back out to the waiting room, where the clerk had more paperwork waiting for her to fill out. She took the clipboard the clerk passed her through the reception window, reclaimed her seat and got to work filling in the blanks and signing her name repeatedly, simultaneously praying that Levi was going to pull through.

At least they had the best health coverage money could buy now. Brandon had seen to that months ago. When she agreed to have the baby, he'd set up a fund that would pay thirty years' worth of premiums for her and the child. At the time, she'd argued that she had Affordable Care and that would be plenty. But he'd insisted that she should have the very best—and that the fund would be set up to cover Levi, too, and any children she ever had.

"Everybody gets sick at some point," Brandon had reminded her softly, a hard truth that he knew all too intimately. "Everybody needs health care at some point. When that happens for you, for the baby or for Levi, you don't need to be worrying about how to pay your share of the hospital bill."

Thank God for Brandon.

Tears searing the back of her throat, Addie signed the last form, got up and passed the clipboard through the window to the clerk. The clerk handed back a couple of forms and her insurance card. She jammed all that in her purse and was pulling out her phone to call her half sister when James Bravo pushed through the emergency room doors.

He came right for her, so big and solid and capable-looking, still wearing the same jeans and chambray shirt with blood on the collar that he'd been wearing when she found him tied up in the basement an hour before. Those blue eyes with the dark rims around the iris were full of concern. "How're you holding up?"

She wanted to lean on him, to have him put his big arms around her and promise her that everything would work out fine. But what gave her the right to go leaning on him? She didn't get it. It was…something he did to her. As if he were a magnet and she were a paper clip. Every time she saw the guy, she felt like just…falling into him, plastering herself against him. She didn't understand it, felt nothing but suspicious of it, of her own powerful attraction to him.

And what made it all even worse was that she seemed to feel he was magnetized to her, too.

Addie didn't have time for indulging in the feelings he stirred in her. She completely distrusted feelings like those and she knew she was right to distrust them. Really, why shouldn't she reject all that craziness that happened between men and women?

Her dad ran off, vanished before she was born, never to be seen or heard from again, just as her sister's dad had done before that, leaving their mother single, pregnant and brokenhearted both times—or so her grandpa always said. Addie had never been able to ask her mom about it. Hannah Kenwright had died giving her life.

So yeah, Addie was cynical about romantic love. And every time she'd tried it, she'd grown only more cynical. Yes, all right. Love had worked out fine for her sister. Still, Addie didn't trust it. To her, romance and all that just seemed like a really stupid and dangerous thing.

And it wasn't as if she hadn't given it her best shot. Three times. In high school and then again when she was twenty-one and finally with a bull rider she'd met at the county rodeo. Her high school love had married someone else and her second forever guy had dumped her flat. The bull rider had dumped her, too, the morning after their first night together. For her, same as for her mother, love had not lasted.

And now she had a baby on the way. And her grandfather to care for. And Red Hill and her horses and a side business she loved. It was enough. She didn't need the human magnet that was James Bravo, thank you very much.

He asked again if she was okay.

"I'm fine," she lied and plastered on a smile. "It's all taken care of. Before he died, Brandon saw to it that we have the kind of insurance that covers everything, no deductibles and no co-pays. So money is no worry. Everything is going to be okay."

He didn't buy that lie. She could see that in those gorgeous eyes of his. But he didn't call her on it. He only asked, "How's Levi?"

"They have him stabilized, they said, and they're flying him to St. Anne's Memorial in Denver for surgery." She dropped her phone in her purse yet again and pulled his out. It was one of those fancy android phones with all the bells and whistles. "I'm sorry. I forgot to give this back to you." She shoved it at him.

He took it. "No problem."

"Thank you. For everything, up to and including *not* having my granddad thrown in jail."

A smile twitched at the corner of his handsome mouth. "You're welcome."

She was just trying to figure out how to tell him gently to get lost, when he continued, "So you need to get to Denver? Come on, I'll drive you."

And then, with no warning, he touched her.

He wrapped his big, warm fingers around her bare

arm right below the short sleeve of her T-shirt, causing a sudden hot havoc of sensation, like little fireworks exploding in a line, up to her shoulder, across to the base of her throat and then straight down to the center of her.

She stood stock-still, gaping up at him, thinking, *Just tell him that you'll manage. Just tell him to let go and leave.*

"Let me drive you." He said it low. Intensely. As if he knew what she was thinking and wouldn't give up until he'd gone and changed her mind.

She demanded, "Don't you have to be in court or something?"

He looked kind of amused—but in a serious and determined way. "Not today. Let me take you to Denver."

She longed to refuse again. But the truth was she needed to get to St. Anne's, and she needed to get there fast. As soon as PawPaw was safely through his surgery, she could figure out the rest.

James watched her face. He still held her arm and he smelled way too good. A little dusty, a little sweaty, with a faint hint of some manly aftershave still lingering even after all her grandpa had put him through. He demanded, "Have you called Carmen?"

"Not yet."

"So it's best to let me take you. You can make all the calls you need to make while we're on the road."

Ten minutes later, they were flying along the state highway on the way to I-25. She called Carmen.

At the sound of her sister's voice, the damn tears started spurting again. "Carm?" she squeaked, all tight and wobbly, both at once.

And Carmen knew instantly that something was wrong. "Omigod, honey, what's happened?"

James reached over in front of her and dropped open the glove box. He pulled out a box of tissues. Was there anything the man wasn't ready for? She whipped out a tissue and dabbed at her eyes. He put the box back and withdrew his big, hard arm.

"Addie Anne. Honey, are you still there?"

"I'm here. I'm okay. It's PawPaw."

"Oh, no. Is he—"

"He had a heart attack, but he's still alive." *At least, he was half an hour ago.* She explained about the helicopter to St. Anne's and the emergency surgery that would happen there.

"But…a heart attack? How…?"

Addie squeezed her eyes shut as she pictured James tied to that chair, Levi yelling and waving his shotgun, the hole he'd blown in the basement ceiling. "Long story." Dear Lord. Was it ever! And Carmen didn't know about the baby yet, either. "I'll fill you in on everything later, promise. But…do you think you can come?"

"Of course I'll come."

Relief flooded through Addie. Times like this, a girl needed her big sister's hand to hold. "I'm so glad."

"I'll be there as soon as I can. St. Anne's, you said?"

"Yeah. I've got nothing but the name of the hospital at this point."

"Don't worry. I'll find you. I can get family leave from work and figure it all out with Devin, see if his mom can come and stay with the kids." Devin's mother had moved to Laramie after her husband died. She'd wanted to be closer to her grandkids. "I'll get everything arranged as fast as I can and then meet you there. Call my cell if…" Carmen faltered and then finished weakly, "If there's any other news."

"I will. Love you, Carm."

"Love you, too…"

They said goodbye. Addie disconnected the call and sagged against the passenger window. Too much was happening. Losing Brandon followed by constant morning sickness had been more than enough for her to handle. She had simply not been prepared to deal with her crazy grandpa kidnapping James Bravo and then having a heart attack on top of the rest. Pressing a hand against her roiling belly, she dabbed at her eyes and willed James's fancy quad cab to get there superfast.

At the hospital, they were sent straight to the surgery wing, where her grandpa was being prepped for bypass surgery. Addie dealt with yet more forms. James took a seat in the waiting room and Addie went in with the surgeon to look at images of Levi's heart and listen to a description of the surgery to come.

James was waiting when she emerged. She knew the sweetest rush of gratitude, just to have him there. He was practically a stranger—or at least, no more than a casual friend—and she needed to remember that. Still, it meant so much to have someone waiting when she left the surgeon and his pictures of her grandpa's blocked-up arteries. It meant the world to her not to have to do this alone.

At the sight of her, he got up and came for her. "Addie," he said. "You're dead white. You need to sit down."

"I can't… I don't…" What was wrong with her words? Why wouldn't they organize themselves into actual sentences?

"Come on now." He reached out and drew her close, into his height and hardness and warmth. "It's going to be all right." She let herself sag against his solid strength. It felt way too good there, pressed tight to his side, his big arm banded around her.

But then her poor stomach started churning again. And this time, she couldn't swallow hard enough or breathe slowly enough to settle it down. With a sharp cry, she pushed James away and ran for the ladies' room.

At least it wasn't far, a quick sprint across the waiting room. She shoved through the door and made for the first stall, knocking the stall door inward with the flat of her hand, flinging back the seat and bracing her palms on her thighs just in time. Everything started coming up as her long hair fell forward, getting in the way. She grabbed for it, trying to shove it back and keep her purse from dropping off her shoulder and spilling all over the floor, too.

And then, suddenly, there was James again, right there in the stall with her, gently gathering her hair and smoothing it back out of the way. God. How humiliating. And this *was* the ladies' room. He shouldn't even be in here.

"It's okay, take it easy. You're okay, okay…" He kept saying that, "You're okay," over and over in that deep, velvety voice of his. She didn't feel okay, not in the least. But she was in no position to argue the point, with all her attention focused on the grim job of ejecting what was left of her lunch.

She gagged for what seemed like such a long, awful time. But then, finally, when there was nothing left inside her poor belly, the retching slowed and stopped. Panting, trying to even out her breathing, she waited to make sure there would be no surprises.

"Better?" he asked, still in that low, gentle, comforting voice.

Addie groaned and nodded. "Would you…?" *Sentences. Whole sentences.* "Go. I'll be all right. Just…go on out. I'll be there in a minute."

"You're sure?"

"Yeah. Uh, thank you. I'm sure." She flushed away the mess and straightened with care, clutching her shoulder bag closer, physically unable to face him right then.

She felt him back from the stall, the warmth and size of him retreating. He said, "I'll be right outside, if you need anything."

"Thank you." She stared, unblinking, at the tan wall above the toilet, willing him to go.

And at last, he did. She heard the door open and shut and instantly released the breath she hadn't realized she'd been holding.

Slowly, with another long sigh, she turned to confront the empty space behind her. On rubbery legs, she went to the sink and rinsed her face and her mouth. At least there were Tic Tacs in her purse. She ate four of them, sucking on them madly, grateful beyond measure for their sharp, minty taste. She brushed her hair and checked her T-shirt for spills. Really, she looked terrible, hollow-eyed and pasty-faced. But at least her stomach had stopped churning now that it was empty.

Note to self: Never eat again—and get out there and tell poor James that you are fine and he can go.

Smoothing her hair one last time and settling her purse strap firmly on her shoulder, she returned to the waiting room.

He was sitting across the room in the row of padded chairs, busy on his fancy phone. She got maybe two steps in his direction before he glanced up and saw her. He jumped to his feet, his handsome, square-jawed face so serious, his beautiful eyes darkened with concern.

For her.

Okay, he really was a good person. And he shouldn't be so concerned about her. He should find himself a nice woman, one who didn't have all her issues, one who believed in true love and forever. Clearly, the guy deserved a woman like that.

She marched right up to him and aimed her chin high. "You have been…amazing. I can't thank you enough for everything. And my sister will be here before you know it, so there isn't any need for you to—"

"Stop." He actually put up a hand. And then he took her by the arm again, causing all those strange, heated sensations to pulse along her skin. "Sit down before you fall down." He took her other arm, too, and then he turned her and carefully guided her down into the chair where he'd been sitting. The chair was warm from his body, and that felt both enormously comforting—and way too intimate, somehow.

Once he had her in the chair, he just stayed there, bent over her, his big hands gripping the chair arms, kind of holding her there, his face with its manly sprouting of five-o'clock shadow so close she could see the faint, white ridge of an old scar on the underside of his chin. It was a tiny scar, and she wondered where he might have gotten it.

She stared up at him, miserable, wishing for a little more gumption when she needed it. "It's not right that you have to be here. It's not fair, after…everything. Given the…situation. James, I'm taking total advantage of you and I hate that."

"You're not. Stop saying you are. I'm here because I want to be here."

She laughed. It was a sad laugh, almost like a sob. "Having a great time, are you?"

"Wonderful."

"Ha!"

He let go of the chair arms and rose to his height. "And you'll feel better if you eat something."

"Oh, no." She pressed a hand to her belly, which still ached a little from the aftermath of losing everything that had been in it, including what felt like a good portion of her stomach lining. "Uh-uh. What I need is never, ever to eat again."

"A little hot tea and some soda crackers. You should be able to keep that down. Then later, I'll get you some soup."

She glared up at him. "What I really hate…"

"Tell me."

"…is that tea and soda crackers sound kind of good."

His fine mouth twitched at the corners. "Sugar?"

"Yes, please. Two packets."

"Don't budge from that chair. I'll be right back."

Addie drank her tea and ate four packets of soda crackers. She felt better after that, and she told James so. He nodded approvingly as he munched on the turkey sandwich he'd brought back from the cafeteria along with her tea and crackers.

Actually, his sandwich looked kind of good, too. She tried not to stare at it longingly.

But the man missed nothing. He chuckled and held out the other half to her.

She should have refused it. It wasn't right to take the guy's food. He was probably starving. She knew *she* was. And just to prove it, her stomach rumbled.

"Take it," he said, those blue eyes all twinkly and teasing. "I know where to get more."

She did take it. Ate it all, too. And felt a whole lot better once she did.

A few minutes after she'd demolished half his sandwich, her cell rang. It was Carm, who said that her mother-in-law was staying with the kids and she and Devin were on the way.

"A couple of hours and we're there," Carmen promised. "How's PawPaw?"

"In surgery, which is going to take at least three hours from what the surgeon said. When you get here, they'll still be operating on him."

"Anything you need?"

She longed for a toothbrush. And she still needed to find someone to take care of Moose and the horses back at the ranch. But she could call her neighbors herself. And she didn't want her sister wasting her time stopping at a drugstore. "Just you. Just get here as fast as you can." Carmen promised she would do exactly that and they said goodbye.

Addie got to work trying to find someone to look after the livestock. But the Fitzgeralds, who had twenty acres bordering Red Hill, were off visiting relatives in Southern California. And Grant Newsome, Levi's longtime friend, had put his house and acreage up for sale and gone to Florida to live near his oldest daughter and her family.

She was trying to figure out who else she might try when James suggested, "How about Walker McKellan? He and his wife, my cousin Rory, would be happy to help. They're not that far from Red Hill." Walker and Rory lived at Walker's guest ranch, the Bar N, which was maybe eight miles from the Red Hill ranch house.

Addie knew Walker, but not that well. He'd been more than a decade ahead of her in school. And Rory was an actual princess from some tiny country in Europe. Addie had met her just once and been impressed with how friendly and down-to-earth she was. "I hardly know them and I'm sure they're busy and don't have time to—"

"Stop," James said again, in the same flat, dismissive

tone he'd used on her when she tried to tell him to go. "*I* know them. And I know they'll want to help. I'm calling them." He had his phone out and ready.

"*You* stop," she insisted, strongly enough that he quit scrolling through his contacts and looked at her with great patience. She added, "I *said* that I hardly know them and it doesn't seem right to take advantage of them."

"It's not taking advantage. It's just asking for help. And there's nothing wrong with asking for help now and then, Addie."

She didn't really have a comeback ready for that one, so she settled for glaring daggers at him.

He gentled his tone. "Look. You'd do the same for them in a heartbeat, wouldn't you?"

"Of course I would, but—"

"So someday they'll need you. And you'll be there. And that's good."

By then, she didn't know why she'd even tried to argue with him. "I bet you could sell an Eskimo a refrigerator," she grumbled.

He shrugged. "Hey, with the way weather patterns are changing, an Eskimo might need one. Ah. Here we go." He punched in the call.

Ten minutes later, she'd talked to both Walker and Rory and they were set to tend to the animals for as long as she needed them to. Walker said he'd take Moose back to the Bar-N. He even insisted she give him the phone numbers of the owners of the horses she boarded. He said he would call them personally and let them know what was happening, reassure them that their animals were being cared for and that if they needed anything, he would see that they got it.

Addie thanked Walker profusely.

He said essentially what James had said. "We should have joined forces years ago for times like this."

When she hung up, she handed James back his phone. "I think I'm running out of ways to thank you."

He didn't miss a beat. "You can thank me by eating the soup I'm going to go get for you now. They have chicken noodle or New England clam chowder."

"No clams. Please."

"Chicken noodle it is, then."

She dug in her purse for her wallet. But he was already up and headed for the elevators.

When he returned with the soup, he also brought sandwiches. Two of them—one roast beef, one ham, both with chips.

She took the soup and tried to give him a ten. He waved it away. She should insist he take the money, but so far, insisting wasn't getting her anywhere with him.

So fine, then. She ate every last drop of that soup and half of his ham sandwich, too. Unfortunately, once the food was gone, there was nothing else to do but sit there and try to read the magazines strewn about the waiting room tables, try *not* to watch the second hand crawling around the face of the clock on the far wall, try not to think too hard about what might be happening down the long hallway beyond the automatic double doors.

Carmen and Devin arrived at a little after nine. Addie ran to her sister. Carmen grabbed her and they hugged each other tight. Then Carmen took her by the shoulders and held her a little away. Carmen was taller and thinner than Addie and her hair was dark brown, her eyes a warm hazel.

"Any news?" her sister asked.

Addie pressed her lips together and shook her head.

"We're still waiting to hear. I'm hoping it won't be too long now."

Devin, tall and lean with light blond hair, said, "Levi's tough as old boots. He'll pull through and be driving us all crazy again in no time."

Addie turned to her brother-in-law. "I know you're right." He hugged her, too. "I can't even tell you how glad I am you're both here." She wrapped an arm around each of them and turned for the row of chairs several feet away where James, on his feet now, was waiting.

Carmen leaned close and whispered, "Isn't that one of the Bravo brothers?"

Addie stifled a tired sigh. "It's James."

"The lawyer, right, second of Sondra's two sons?"

Addie nodded. "He was, um, there when PawPaw had the heart attack. He's been wonderful," she whispered back grimly, reminded again of all the news she needed to share with her sister. "I can't get him to leave."

"I heard that," James said wryly. "Carmen, Devin. How have you been?" He held out his big hand.

Devin took it first, and then Carmen. Carmen said how grateful she was for his help. She assured him he could go now.

He just shook his head. "I can't go now. I wouldn't feel right. At least not until Levi's through surgery."

Carmen shot Addie a look and then turned to him again. "You and our grandfather are…friends?"

"Well, we've kind of formed a bond, I think you might say."

Now Carmen glanced at Devin, who shrugged, then back to James and finally at Addie. "Okay. What is going on?"

Addie groaned. "Got a month, I'll tell you everything."

"I'm here and I'm listening," Carmen replied.

Addie hardly knew where to start.

James got up. "I could use some coffee. Anybody else?"

Carmen piped right up. "I'll take some." She elbowed her husband. "Dev will go with you."

"Uh. I will?" When Carmen elbowed him again, Devin caught on. "Sure. Great idea."

"Tea?" Addie asked James, and then got uncomfortable all over again thinking how easily she'd started to depend on him.

"You got it—and maybe Devin and I will hang around the cafeteria for a while." He gave her a look—one thick, dark eyebrow raised.

And she took his meaning. "Go ahead. Tell him," she said. "Tell him everything you know. Believe me, he won't be surprised."

"My God," murmured Carmen. "What *is* going on?" For that, she got another bewildered shrug from her husband.

James asked, "You sure?"

Addie nodded. "He has to know eventually anyway."

So the men left. And Carmen said, "Okay. Tell me everything."

Addie told all—from how she'd agreed to have Brandon's baby, to the fact that she was now pregnant with said baby, to Levi snooping in her trash and finding the test stick and then kidnapping James just the way he'd done to Devin eight years ago. Carmen sat there with her mouth hanging open, as Addie went on to describe finding James and Levi in the basement and the shotgun going off, blowing a hole in the ceiling while Levi had a heart attack.

Finally, when the totally out-there story was told,

Carmen hugged her again and told her she loved her and could hardly believe she was going to be an auntie.

Then came the questions. "If Brandon's the father, why did PawPaw kidnap James?"

"He won't believe it's Brandon. He claims he's seen the way James and I look at each other and he just knows there's been a lot more than looking going on."

Carmen was silent. Too silent.

Addie was forced to demand, "What is all this *silence* about, Carm?"

"Well, now, honey. I did see the way you and James looked at each other just now…"

"What are you talking about? I swear to you, James Bravo has never done more than shake my hand—at least not until today, when he put his arm around me to comfort me, held my hair while I threw up and then made me sit down when I tried to get him to leave."

"But that's just it, see?"

"No, I don't see."

"He seems very devoted. And I saw the blood on his collar."

"I told you, PawPaw knocked him out, tied him to a chair in the basement and put a shotgun to his head. Because you know PawPaw. He thinks we live in some Wild West romance novel where it's perfectly okay to hold a man at gunpoint in order to convince him to 'do the right thing.'" She said that with air quotes.

Carm snickered and then quickly switched to a more sober expression. "And yet, even after all the abuse Paw-Paw heaped on the poor guy, James drives you to Denver and holds your hair while you hurl? He knows you're having another man's baby, but he brings you food and tea and insists he has to stay with you to make sure that your crazy old grandpa makes it through surgery?"

"Carm, it's not like that. It's just that he's a good guy."

"Beyond stellar, apparently."

"Really, I hardly know him. We…well, we talk now and then."

A sideways look from Carmen. "You talk."

"Yeah. He's bought land that borders Red Hill and he's building a house there. I go by there a lot, working with the horses, you know?"

"Right…"

"Quit looking at me like that. Sometimes I stop is all. We visit. We talk about life and stuff—in general, I mean. Nothing all that personal." Well, okay. Once, James had told her about his ex-wife. But as a rule, they kept it casual. She added, "And now and then, he drops by the ranch house. We sit out under the stars and chat."

"Chat," Carmen repeated, as though the simple word held a bunch of other meanings that Addie wasn't admitting to.

"Yeah." Addie straightened her shoulders. "Chat. Just chat. And that's it. That's all. I've never gone out with him. It's casual and it's only conversation and you couldn't even really call us friends."

Carmen patted her hand. "I'm only saying I'm not surprised that PawPaw jumped to conclusions."

Addie batted off her sister's touch. "It is Brandon's baby. I have never even kissed James Bravo."

Carmen put up both hands. "Okay, okay. I believe you."

"Oh, gee. Thanks a bunch." Addie pressed a hand to her stomach, which had started churning again.

Carmen hooked an arm around her shoulders and drew her close. "And I don't want you upset." She stroked Addie's hair. It felt really good. Carmen was only two years older, but Addie had always looked up to her. When you grow up without a mom, a good big sister really helps. Carmen chided, "It's bad for the baby, for you to get so upset."

"No kidding." Grudgingly, Addie leaned her head on her big sister's shoulder.

"Just breathe and relax. We're going to get through this. PawPaw is going to be fine—and here come the guys."

Addie glanced up and saw that James and Devin had just come around the corner from the elevators. "I don't like the way you say *the guys*. Like James is suddenly part of the family."

"Honey, stop overreacting. It's only going to make you want to throw up."

Well, okay. That was true. And Carmen was right. They just needed to stay calm and support each other. There'd been more than enough drama today to last Addie a lifetime.

So she focused on speaking softly, on being grateful—for her sister and Devin. And yes, for James, too. He'd made a horrible time a lot less awful and she needed to remember how much she owed him.

She drank her tea and ate the toast James had brought her. Strangely enough, she'd kept more food down in the past few hours than she had in days. Yet another reason to be grateful to James.

When she finished her tea and toast, she realized she was completely exhausted. She leaned her head back against the wall behind her and closed her eyes just for a minute.

The next thing she knew, James was rubbing her arm, stroking her hair, whispering in her ear, "Addie, wake up. The doctor's coming…"

With a sharp cry she sat bolt upright—and realized she'd been sound asleep, her head on James's broad shoulder. The big clock on the far wall showed that over an hour had passed since she leaned back and closed her eyes.

And James was right.

Levi's surgeon had emerged from the long hallway between the double doors and was coming right for them.

Chapter Three

They all popped to their feet at once—James, Addie, Carmen and Devin. And then they waited in a horrible, breath-held silence until the doctor, still in surgical scrubs with a matching cap on his head and a mask hanging around his neck, reached them and started speaking.

Addie watched his mouth move and tried to listen to what he was saying, but her heart was beating so damn loud and her blood made a whooshing sound as it spurted through her body and the words were really hard to understand.

But then Carm said, "Oh, thank God."

And Addie put it together: he'd made it. PawPaw had survived the surgery.

Forty-five minutes later, they all proceeded to a new waiting room, this one adjacent to the Cardiac Surgery

Intensive Care Unit, which was five floors up from surgery and in another wing.

A nurse came out and led Addie and Carmen through automatic doors and down a hall to one of those rooms full of curtained cubicles. In this room, all the curtains were drawn back. There were twenty beds, two rows of ten, half of them with patients in them. Nurses, doctors and technicians moved between the beds and back and forth from the group of desks that formed a command center in the middle of the room. The nurse led them to the left side of the room, the third bed from the door. Addie clutched for Carm's hand and when she got it, she held on tight.

Levi lay on the hospital bed with a tube down his throat and another in his nose. There were tubes and wires hooked to his chest, and more of them disappearing under the blankets. And there was an IV in the back of his hand and another in the crook of his arm. Both arms were strapped to the bed; Addie assumed that was to keep him from pulling out any of the complicated apparatus that hooked him up to the various machines. There was a ventilator by the bed. It wheezed softly as it pushed air in through the tube in his mouth.

He looked terrible, every line in his craggy face dug in deeper than before. But he did open his eyes briefly. It seemed he saw them, recognized them. But then a second later, his eyelids drooped shut. Together, still clutching each other's hands, Addie and Carm moved closer, up to the head of the bed. Gently, so lightly, Addie dared to touch his pale forehead below the blue cap that covered his hair.

He groaned and opened his eyes again.

Carm touched his wiry upper arm at a rare spot where no tube or needle was stuck. "I'm here, PawPaw. We're both here. You made it through your surgery and you're going to get well."

"We love you," said Addie, biting back tears. "We love you so much."

His red-rimmed blue eyes tracked—from Addie, to Carmen, back to Addie again. And then he tried to speak. "Aiff. Air aiff?"

Carm said, "Shh, don't try to talk now. The tube's in the way."

But he wouldn't shush. "Aiff? Ear? Aiff?" He tried to lift an arm, found it pinned to the bed and groaned in frustration.

Addie stroked his brow. "Shh, PawPaw. Don't. You'll only hurt your throat."

The nurse who'd brought them in approached again. Addie and Carmen stepped back and the nurse bent close to Levi. "Easy, now, Levi. It's okay. We'll find out what you want and get it for you. I've got a pencil and a paper…" She pulled a small tablet and a pencil out of her pocket.

He nodded, making a harsh gargling sound around the tube.

"Is he left-handed?" she asked.

Carm said, "No, right-handed."

The nurse eased the tablet under his right hand and wrapped his scarred, knotted old fingers around the pencil. He gripped it and scratched at the paper.

When he stopped, the nurse asked, "Is that it?"

Levi grunted a yes.

The nurse took the tablet and read, "Jane? You want to see Jane?"

Another grunt accompanied by a head shake.

Addie knew. "James," she said bleakly. "You want James."

More grunting, but this time with a nod. Her grandpa stared right at her, daring her to produce the man he demanded to see.

She turned away—and there was Carm, looking all innocent, giving a little "what can you do about it?" shrug.

"Fine," Addie said and tried not to sound as fed up as she felt. "I'll get him."

Levi grunted again. To Addie, the sound was way too triumphant.

The nurse took her out and waited by the double doors.

Devin and James jumped to their feet again at the sight of her. She marched up to James, blew out a breath of pure frustration and said, "I'm sorry. He's asking to see you."

"Uh. Sure."

"I hate to ask you to go in there."

"I don't mind. Honestly, I don't."

"It only encourages him in his ridiculous delusions."

James held her eyes steadily. "Addie. Right now we just want him happy and calm, right?"

"Yeah. But what if you weren't here?"

"But I am here."

And you shouldn't be. But she didn't say that out loud. Because he'd been a lifesaver and she was so grateful to him it made an ache down in the heart of her. She turned to Devin. "Don't be hurt that PawPaw didn't ask for you. You know he thinks the world of you."

"I'm not hurt." Dev seemed to mean it. "I'm just glad he's pulled through the surgery all right." He clapped James on the shoulder. "Good luck, man."

James made a low noise in his throat that could have meant anything and fell in beside Addie as she marched back to where the nurse waited to lead them through the double doors.

In CSICU, Carm stood by the bed holding Levi's hand. His eyes were shut. But he must have heard their footsteps, because, with obvious effort, he opened them again and focused instantly in on James.

"Levi," James said mildly. "See? I'm right here and I'm going nowhere." Addie gasped and shot him a sharp look, but he kept his gaze on Levi as he softly added, "Rest now."

Levi blinked a couple of times, as if to reassure himself that his old eyes and his drugged mind weren't playing any tricks on him. Then, with a low, rough sound of pure satisfaction, he closed his eyes and didn't open them again, though the three of them stood there for several more minutes. Finally, the nurse bustled over and whispered that it was time to go. They would be allowed back in for brief visits—no more than two of them at a time, please—for as long as Levi stayed in intensive care.

They filed back out to the waiting room, where Carmen went straight to Devin. She sagged against him. He gathered her in and stroked her hair as Addie told herself she was not, under any circumstances, going to sidle up close to James and hope that he might wrap those big arms around her.

James said, "I've got a room at the Marriott down the street. I figure we can take turns using it. For showers, naps, whatever."

Carm beamed at him from her husband's arms. "Great idea. Addie should go first. She looks dead on her feet."

Addie sent her sister a quelling glance and asked James, "When did you have time to get a room at the Marriott?"

All twinkly blue eyes and easy charm, he coaxed, "Come on, don't look so suspicious. I made a phone call when you two went in to see Levi. The Marriott had rooms available—you know, being a hotel and all? So I got us one."

He'd done way more than she should have let him do and she needed to put an end to it. Immediately. "We have to talk."

He frowned. "Now, Addie—"

"Go ahead," said Carm with a shooing motion. "You two work it out. We'll be right here."

Addie so didn't like the way Carm had shooed her—as if she and James had had some lovers' spat they needed to resolve. But she could deal with her sister later. Now she and James had to get a few things straight.

She whirled and marched across the waiting room to a grouping of chairs along the other wall. When she got there, she dropped into one.

James took his sweet time following, but finally he sat down next to her. "What's the problem now?"

She turned and met his beautiful eyes and said sincerely, "It's enough—no, it's too much, all you've done. And I thank you so much for everything. But my grandfather's out of surgery now. You said yourself that you were only staying to see that he made it through all right. Well, he has. And Carm and Devin are here, to help me. You don't need to stay anymore."

He studied her face for several nerve-racking seconds. Then he shook his head. "I've reconsidered."

Somehow she made herself ask him quietly, "Reconsidered what?"

"Levi wants me here. And he needs to have what he wants—at least until he's out of the woods."

"But he *is* out of the woods."

"Addie. He's almost eighty. He's just been through major surgery. You know you want him relaxed and focused on getting well. You don't want anything preying on his mind."

Okay, that was true. She didn't want PawPaw upset. But sometimes, well, people just didn't get things the way they wanted them. "I can't help it if he insists on lying to himself." She blew out a hard breath. "Uh-uh. He needs to accept that he's got it all wrong and get past his totally out-there assumption that you are the father of my baby. As long as you're here, that's not going to happen. As long as you're here, he can tell himself his crazy-ass plan to marry us at gunpoint is working the same as it worked when he pulled it on Dev and Carmen."

"So what if he tells himself his plan is working?"

She was gaping again. She'd been doing way too much of that recently. "What do you mean, so what? His plan is *not* working. It's never going to work. You are not my baby's daddy and PawPaw needs to learn to accept that."

"And he will. When he's ready. But he's not ready now. All I'm saying is let me help. Let him believe what he needs to believe until he's back on his feet."

God. He was not only big and strong and kind and helpful, with that killer smile and those damn twinkly eyes. He not only looked good and smelled way too manly and tempting. He was also so calm and logical. And what he said actually seemed to make a bizarre kind of sense.

And she was so darn tired. She kept thinking of that room he'd taken at the Marriott. Of a shower and clean sheets and a few hours of much-needed sleep.

He leaned closer, filling her tipped-over world with his strength and his steadiness. "Come on, Addie." His deep, smooth voice washed through her, so soothing, making her want to lean into him, to curl into a ball and cuddle up close. "Let me help you. I *want* to help you."

"Why?"

The question seemed to hang in the charged air between them.

And then he actually answered it. "I like it, helping you. I honestly do. I like Levi and I want him to get well."

"Even after what he did to you?"

James chuckled. "He's a determined old guy. I admire that. I'm not crazy about his methods, but his intentions are good."

She almost laughed. "What's that they say about good intentions paving the road to hell?"

"Addie, lighten up."

"You shouldn't make excuses for him."

"I'm not. And it's not really all that complicated, or it doesn't have to be. I'll just hang around for a few days, help out however I can, until your grandfather's better."

"Define *better*."

He dodged right on by that one. "Can't we just play that by ear, see how he does?"

"I don't…get what *you* get out of this. I really don't. It's not fair to you, to take advantage of you this way."

His square jaw hardened. "Didn't we already clear up the whole 'taking advantage' question when you finally let Walker and Rory help you out with the animals? No one is taking advantage of me. I'm doing what I want to do. And that is to be here and help out however I can. I *like* helping out."

She really needed just to say it outright and she knew that she did. "You do get that you and me, that's never going to happen, right? I've got a whole lot to deal with in my life right now, and a man is the last thing I need."

He leaned even closer. Every nerve in her body went on red alert. "I do get that, Addie. Yes." Something deep inside her ached with loss when he said that. Which was absurd. It was a simple fact and they needed to be on the same page about it. And then he smiled, so slow and sweet and tender. "Nothing is going to happen. Not unless you ask me real nice."

Warmth slithered through her, followed immediately by annoyance. "Oh, very funny."

"Was I funny?" he teased. "I didn't *mean* to be funny…"

"This isn't a joke."

"And I wasn't joking." His voice was so serious. His eyes were not.

She decided she'd better just let it go. "Good, then. Hold that thought. And…well, you need to remember that I'm *pregnant*, James." She thought of Brandon then, with a sharp ache of loss. Brandon, too thin, too pale, the light fading from his green eyes. She made herself put it right out there, blunt as you please. "I'm pregnant with my dead best friend's baby."

"I am very clear on that." He took her hand. His was so warm and big and strong. It felt way too good and she should pull away.

But she didn't.

Across the waiting area, Carm was watching her, a sly smile on her face.

That did it. Addie tried to jerk free.

But James held on. "Hey."

"What?"

"I want to help and I think you could use the support. It doesn't have to mean anything more than that."

"But you know that it does. People…think we're together. My grandpa is still sure of that. And Carm thinks so, too, and so does Dev."

"So…?"

She did pull her hand from his then. "Do you need *everything* spelled out for you?"

He just wouldn't give up. "Look at me. In my eyes."
The man was impossible.

She puffed out her cheeks with a hard breath. "I don't
think that's such a good idea."

"Come on…"

"Fine." She met that gorgeous blue gaze. "What?"

"It's so simple. I want to be here and I don't expect
anything from you. Can't you just take my word on that?"

Why not just let him stay?

He wanted to help and she liked having him here. She
felt…safe and protected with him around. No, it couldn't
go anywhere. And yeah, the way he hovered over her,
taking care of her, gave her family the wrong idea. But
if it made PawPaw happy right now, if it took a load off
his mind when he needed to be focused on getting well…

How could that be bad, really? How could that possibly hurt?

She groused, "You're way too convincing."

He seemed amused. "You mentioned that before."

"Yeah, well, I'd hate to see you in court. You're probably responsible for a whole bunch of murderers getting
off scot-free."

He gave her that smile of his, the one that warmed her
up from her head to her toes and just about everywhere
in between. "I'm in business and family law. Trusts and
estates, real estate, asset protection. Not a single mur-
derer ever got off because of me."

"I am so relieved to hear it."

He leaned closer. "So, then. Are you going to let me
stay?"

She made a humphing sound. "Is there any way I can
get rid of you?"

He pretended to think it over. "Nope. Give it up.

There's no way I'm leaving, not until I'm sure you don't need me anymore."

What if I never stop needing you? The crazy question just popped into her head.

And she quickly banished it. Because it really wasn't a question of need. Uh-uh. Not at all. She didn't need him. She didn't need any man. She could take care of herself and her coming baby just fine on her own. They'd get through this rough patch, get her grandfather back on his feet, and her life would go back to the way it had always been.

James didn't even wait for her to say he could stay, just went right on as though it was all settled—which, she supposed, it was. "I think your sister is right. You should get some rest. Let me take you to the hotel and get you settled in."

"I hate to leave Carm and Dev here to deal with everything on their—"

"Shh." He put a finger to her lips, so lightly, causing a bunch of silly butterflies to start flapping their wings low in her belly. "You'll be right down the street. Carmen can call you if there's any news."

Addie gave in and confessed, "I am kind of tired…"

He took her hand again. "Come on. You'll be rested and back here at the hospital before you know it."

Ten minutes later, James accepted four key cards from the desk clerk and handed one to Addie.

She took it and looked down at it as though she wondered what to do with it. The woman was dead on her feet.

He took her arm. "Come on. Let's get you to the room."

She glanced up at him then, big bronze eyes rimmed

in shadows—and full of questions. "You're going up with me?"

"Just to see that you're all set. Then I'll head back to Justice Creek."

Her smooth forehead crinkled with a frown. "So... you're leaving, after all?" Did she look kind of hurt? After all that resistance, she really did want him to stay?

That pleased him, probably more than he should allow it to. "Addie, I'm coming right back. I'll just go home, grab a shower and toss a few things in a bag. I'll stop by Red Hill, too. If you give me a key and a list, I'll bring you anything you need."

She stared up at him for a long count of ten after he stopped speaking. Finally, she said, "That would be amazing, if you would do that." Her eyes were almost gold right then. He wished they might shine like that for him all the time—and he started pulling her toward the elevators before she could find something new to argue about. Then she asked, "Can we stop in the gift shop so I can get a toothbrush, please?"

He looked down into her upturned face and never wanted to look away. "The gift shop it is."

"This is a suite," she accused when he pushed the door inward and she saw there was a sitting room. "You didn't need to go and get a suite."

"Too late now." He pulled her in and shut the door. "Sorry, there are only two bedrooms. The presidential suite has three, but it's booked. I thought Carmen and Devin could take one and you and I can make it work with the other. I'll be going back and forth from home anyway." He waited for her to argue that no way she was sharing a room with him.

But instead she said, "I will pay the bill for this room." It wasn't a question.

"It's already handled. Don't worry about it."

"It's not right."

"Sure it is."

"But—"

He cut her off with a wave of his hand. "Let it go. Please."

She started to speak again, seemed to reconsider and then said, "I just don't have the energy to keep arguing about this."

"So don't."

At that, she gave a tired little chuckle. And then, shaking her head, she wandered into the living area and dropped onto the couch, plunking her purse and her gift shop bag on the wide, button-tucked gray ottoman in front of her. "I could sleep for a week." With a groan, she planted her face in her hands.

He sat down beside her, hooked an arm around her shoulders and pulled her close. She stiffened at first, but then she gave in, drooping against him the way she had done in the waiting room when she fell asleep during Levi's surgery. He really liked having her there, tucked in nice and cozy against his side, so he leaned back into the cushions, pulling her right along with him.

She sighed. "I meant what I said about you and me."

"That we're not happening?"

"Yeah. But still…"

He smoothed her hair. "Go ahead. I can take it."

She made a thoughtful sound low in her throat. "Well, I just can't believe your wife let you get away."

He resisted the urge to press a kiss to the crown of her head. "Addie. What a nice thing to say."

"I couldn't stop myself. You really are being completely wonderful."

"Happy to help." He was thinking of those evenings they'd sat talking on the front steps at the Red Hill ranch house. On one of those nights, a bitter cold one not long after Christmas, they'd sat outside in heavy jackets and warm gloves drinking hot chocolate that she'd whipped up for them. That night, he'd told her that he'd been married.

He and Vicki Kelley had tied the knot when he was just starting law school.

Vicki…

He'd been head over heels for Vicki. She was smokin' hot, a real firecracker in bed. She was also extremely possessive. And with rules. Lots and lots of rules.

Vicki didn't like his friends or his family. For the three years of their marriage, he did what Vicki wanted and avoided all the other people who mattered in his life. By the time it ended, he'd pretty much come to the conclusion that marriage wasn't worth it, that a man gave up too much when he tried to make a life with a woman. After Vicki, he'd never gotten anywhere near the altar again. He kept his relationships casual and fun. And when they stopped being one or the other, he would end it as quickly and gently as possible.

Addie sighed again. He stroked her arm and tried not to think too hard about what, exactly, he wanted from her.

That night when he'd told her about his marriage, he'd also said he would never get married again. She'd laughed and said she understood that. She was never getting married, period.

He'd said he didn't get it. Most everyone was willing to give marriage a try at least once, weren't they?

She said she'd had rotten luck with men and she just

didn't want to go there. He'd tried to coax more out of her on the subject. But that was all she would say.

Somehow, in the past few months, he was constantly thinking about her. About her smile and her thick strawberry hair, her round cheeks and curvy body. About the scent of her that was somehow just right, all sweet and sexy and fresh and feminine. About how she said what was on her mind. About how she behaved as though she liked him, but she'd always somehow made it so he never quite got a chance to ask her out. He should probably get smart and take a hint. Hadn't she just told him for the second time tonight that nothing would be happening between them?

And still he refused to believe her.

She was having Brandon Hall's baby. That ought to serve as something of a turnoff.

Nope. He was still hot for her. He hadn't been this attracted to a woman since Vicki.

And look how that turned out.

He said, "I thought I told you that by the end of it, my ex-wife didn't have much appreciation for my many sterling qualities."

Addie tipped her head back and gave him a tired smile. "You did tell me that. And I'm sorry it didn't work out."

"I'm pretty much over it. It was a long time ago." Reluctantly, he reminded her, "And I should get on the road."

She ducked free of his hold and sat forward, leaving his arms feeling empty without her. "You sure it's not too much, stopping by the ranch house?"

He pulled out his phone and brought up the memo app. "Just tell me what you want and where to find it."

After James left, Addie took a shower and brushed her teeth. In her bra and panties, she set the bedside clock to give her two hours of sleep and climbed between the soft white sheets. Not that she expected any sleeping to happen. She just knew she would end up lying there wide-awake, worrying about Levi.

The alarm went off what seemed like five minutes later. She whacked the off button to stop the noise and realized she'd conked right out and slept straight through.

Dragging herself to her feet, she trudged to the bathroom and splashed water on her face. Then she combed her hair, pulled on her clothes and returned to the hospital.

Carmen said that they'd just been in to see him. "They took out the breathing tube, so he's breathing on his own."

"He asked about James again," Devin reported in a wary tone.

"He said he wanted to talk to James," Carmen added gingerly.

"Talk to James about what?" Addie demanded and tried not to sound hostile. It wasn't Carm's fault that their grandfather had a screw loose when it came to James.

Carmen winced. "About the, um, wedding."

Chapter Four

A low noise rose from Addie's throat. She realized as she made it that it sounded a whole lot like a growl. "What wedding? There's no wedding."

Carm put on her innocent face. "Ahem, well, apparently, PawPaw thinks that you and James are getting married."

Addie drew three slow breaths through her nose and then said with quiet reasonableness, "PawPaw has it all wrong."

"Well, we know that," said Carmen. "We're only telling you what *he* said—and where *is* James, by the way?"

"He went home to pick up a few things."

"But he's coming back?"

"Carm. You are altogether too concerned about what James Bravo is doing."

"Well, I like him. He's a great guy and at a time like this, it's good to have someone like him around. Is that so wrong?"

Dev jumped right to Carm's defense, wrapping an arm around her, pressing a husbandly kiss at her temple. "I like him, too. The man is solid."

Addie looked from Dev to Carm and back to Dev again. "You both get that none of this is his problem, right? You get that he's only helping out from the goodness of his heart. And why he could find any goodness there for PawPaw, I haven't a clue. Not after what PawPaw did to him. James owes us nothing. Get that? Not. A. Thing."

Carmen sniffed. "Sheesh, Addie Anne. Defensive much?"

"I just need to make that stubborn old man see the light, that's all."

"Not right this minute, you don't," Carmen argued. "Right this minute, he doesn't need anything upsetting him. He needs to rest and get better."

Addie got that. She did. She just hated the idea of allowing their grandfather to continue in his delusion that James was the father of her baby. Worse, he was completely locked in to the idea that James's imagined paternity automatically meant she and James needed to be married.

It was so stupid. *Earth to PawPaw. The 1950s called and they would like their rigid moral standards back.*

And how was her standing here arguing about it with her sister and brother-in-law going to help PawPaw see the light?

It wasn't.

She gave them the key to the suite, explained that the unused bedroom was theirs and told them to go get some rest.

Once they were gone, she used the phone on the wall by the double doors to check with the nurses' station.

They said Levi was resting and, yes, she could come in and sit by his bed.

She spent an hour in there, just watching him sleep. He looked so sick and frail. It broke her heart to see him that way.

But then he opened his eyes and the first word out of his mouth was a raspy "James?"

She bent closer to him. "Shh, now," she whispered, way too aware of the other patients trying to sleep nearby, of the other patients' relatives, sitting quietly in the dark. "Rest, PawPaw. Get your strength back."

"Where is he?"

"It doesn't matter. He's got nothing to do with you."

"I want to talk to him."

"Shh. You'll wake the other patients."

He grabbed her hand, his grip surprisingly strong, given that he'd just been through open-heart surgery. "You get him in here." The machines hooked up to him started making insistent beeping noises as the fluorescent green rows of wavy patterns leaped and dipped across the heart monitor screen over the bed.

"He's not here." She jerked her hand free of his grip. "PawPaw, settle down."

Two nurses hustled over. One bent over Levi as the other spoke softly to Addie, "He's going to be fine. Come on with me."

Out in the waiting room, the nurse reassured her that they would give her grandfather something to relax him. She wanted to know what had agitated him.

Addie gave a hopeless shrug. "I don't even know where to start."

"Whatever you can tell us will help us to help him."

She gave in and told the nurse that she was pregnant and her grandfather refused to accept who the father was but had fixated on someone else and was determined to make her the wrong guy's shotgun bride. "In the, um, figurative sense, of course," she hastened to add and felt her silly cheeks flaming at the lie.

"Of course," the nurse repeated. Because it was the twenty-first century and everybody knew that there were no *real* shotgun brides anymore.

"My grandfather wants to talk to the guy he *thinks* is the father. He's just sure he can get the poor man to give in and marry me—even though I've told him repeatedly that he's got it all wrong. And that's not even taking into account the fact that I have no intention of marrying anyone."

The nurse listened patiently and then suggested, "Maybe the best thing is to leave him to us for the night. We'll keep him calm and make sure he gets the rest he needs."

What could she do but agree? "Okay. But I'll be right here in the waiting room—either me or my sister."

The nurse reassured her that she would be notified immediately if there was any change in Levi's condition. And then she said that she was sure everything would work out and Levi would soon come to accept that he needed to stop upsetting himself and focus on his recovery.

Addie fervently hoped that the nurse had it right.

The nurse returned to ICU and Addie went over and dropped into a chair. Her phone, which she'd set on vibrate, buzzed from the outer pocket of her purse.

It was James. "I'm on my way. About twenty minutes out. Where are you?"

Her silly heart leaped. She really shouldn't be so overjoyed just to hear his voice, to know he was coming, that he would be here soon. "I'm at the hospital."

"Did you get any rest at all?"

"I did, yes." She forced a little brightness into her tone. "Two whole hours. I was out like a light. I got back here to the hospital about an hour and a half ago and sent Carmen and Dev back to the hotel."

"How's your grandfather doing?"

"He's fine. They've got him resting comfortably." It wasn't a lie, exactly. The nurse had promised they would quiet him down. "You should go straight to the hotel. Get a little sleep."

"I'll see you in a few minutes."

"Did you hear what I said, James?"

"Every word." He sounded amused, which annoyed her no end. "Gotta go. See you in a few."

"James?"

But he'd already hung up.

James came around the corner from the bank of elevators and saw Addie alone in the CSICU waiting room reading a paperback book.

He hung back for a moment and just looked at her. She had her elbows on the chair arms, her bright head bent to the page, legs crossed, one booted foot bouncing a little. He smiled at the sight.

That was the thing about Addie. Most times, just the sight of her made the day—or in this case, the middle of the night—seem a whole light brighter.

As he stood there and grinned, she suddenly looked up and caught sight of him. Those big eyes softened—but only for a second. Then she pursed up her mouth at him. Because he'd been watching her unawares? Because he hadn't followed her instructions and gone to the hotel? Who knew?

And it didn't matter. Whatever her mood, he liked to look at her.

He went and claimed the chair next to her. "Good book?"

"Yeah, as a matter of fact." She flashed him the battered cover, which showed a passionately embracing, nearly naked couple, both with seriously '80s hair. "I read it years ago. It was in my mother's stash of romances in the closet of her old room. Carm and I read them all."

"So…now you're reading it again?"

She shrugged. "I found this copy under that chair against the far wall. Just the sight of it made me smile. It's about this teacher who takes a job in North Dakota in the early 1900s. She meets this grouchy farmer. They're always bickering. It's funny. And sweet. Made me cry, too. And right about now, I'm grateful for anything that takes my mind off my burning desire to strangle my grandfather."

Apparently, something had happened with Levi. Why wasn't he surprised? "Come on, whatever he did, it can't be that bad. He's barely out of surgery. He doesn't have the strength to make trouble."

She slanted him a glance—and then muttered, "You'd be surprised. He's so unbelievably stubborn. He gets some crazy idea in his head and he won't give it up no matter what."

James waited for her to get more specific. When she didn't, he asked, "And this crazy idea he won't give up is…?"

She bit her soft lower lip and shook her head. "Take a wild guess."

Guessing wasn't necessary. "He still thinks I'm the baby's father and he wants us married now or sooner."

"It is so wrong on so many levels."

"Hey." He waited until she turned her head and met his eyes. "How about if, tomorrow, when he's feeling better, I try to talk to him?"

Her round cheeks went bright red. "Are you kidding? That's what he wants. To get you in there and beat up on you. He's just so certain you're going to see the light and say you'll marry me—as if I'm waiting around in a white dress for you to finally agree to make an honest woman of me." She shook her head some more. "Uh-uh. No way are you going in there and dealing with him. He's going to have to wake up and face reality. That's all there is to it."

The next day, when Levi refused to start drinking clear liquids until he'd spoken with James, Addie tried to hold firm.

But they all ganged up on her. The nurses said that if James was willing to quietly discuss the matter with Levi, it could be helpful. Surely he might as well try to make the old man see reason. Carm and Dev agreed with the nurses. Why shouldn't James try? What could it hurt? Maybe James could get through to him. *Somebody* had to.

Addie said, "Oh, please. You know him. When he's like this, there is no way to get through to him. He's locked in to what he's so sure is right. He will do anything—*anything*—to accomplish his goal. It's a sickness, when he gets like this. And trying to talk to him, to humor him, to get him to see things differently? None of that will work. We just need to hold firm."

And then James said, all calm and noble and gratingly sure of himself and his charm and his talent for making people do things *his* way, "I would like to try."

Addie elbowed him in the side when he said that. "I

CHRISTINE RIMMER 69

told you. Weren't you listening? You trying to reason with him will only make him surer that if he keeps pushing, we're going to give in."

"Oh, come on, Addie Anne," Carm pleaded. "At least James can *try*."

"No," Addie said again.

But they wouldn't listen. Ten minutes later, James went through the double doors.

Addie had to hand it to him. He stayed in there a long time. But when he finally came out, she could tell right away from the look on his face that the conversation had only made things worse.

"At least I got him to drink some broth and eat a little Jell-O," he said sheepishly when she and Carm and Dev surrounded him and asked what had happened.

But Addie wasn't reassured. She looked James straight in the eye—and his gaze kind of slid to the side. "Okay. You'd better tell me now. What did you do, James?"

He sank to a chair. "He's just so relentless. And he looks so sick and I…well, I couldn't stand it, all right? I hated to see him like that."

Addie demanded for the second time, "What did you *do*?"

James braced his elbows on his knees and put his head in his hands. "I ended up promising him I would talk to you."

Glances were flying. Carm looked at Addie. Addie looked at Dev. Dev shrugged in confusion and frowned at James.

Addie's stomach lurched alarmingly. "You told him you'd *talk* to me?"

James looked absolutely miserable. "Yeah. I, well, that was how I got him to drink the broth."

Somehow she kept her voice even and reasonable as she inquired, "Talk to me about what?"

"Er, the wedding?"

Dead silence. Then Dev said, "Man. Seriously?"

Addie pressed a hand to her churning belly and asked very softly, "What wedding?"

James dropped his hands between his spread knees, sagged back in the chair and groaned at the ceiling. "*Our* wedding."

That did it for Addie. "I'll be right back." She clapped her hand over her mouth and ran for the ladies' room.

"Addie?" Carm called from behind her, close on her heels.

Addie didn't turn. She didn't dare. She knocked the door wide with the heel of her hand and made for the stall.

Addie needed him. James leaped to his feet. He started to follow after the women.

Devin grabbed his arm. "Hold on, man. Let Carm take care of her. She'll be okay."

James knew Dev was right. He collapsed into the chair again. "It seemed like a good idea at the time, you know? Just to humor him…"

Dev took the chair next to him. "So you told Levi the baby was yours?"

"Hell, no!" He said it way too loud. A couple of old ladies waiting together in the chairs across the room stopped whispering and glared at him. "Sorry," he said. They glared a few seconds more for good measure and went back to their low conversation.

Dev clapped him on the shoulder. "No offense, dude. Just trying to understand what's going on here."

James leaned his head against the wall. It pressed on

the bump back there—the one Levi had made when he coldcocked him the day before. He winced and sat forward, bracing his forearms on his knees. "Maybe we'd just better wait until Addie and Carmen get back."

Dev grunted. "Yeah. No point in going through it all twice."

"Thanks," James said wearily. His phone vibrated. He took it out and checked it. The emails were piling up and he needed to call the office.

Later.

He and Dev waited in a grim yet companionable silence until Addie and Carmen emerged from the ladies' room.

James asked, "You okay?" when Addie sat down next to him. Carmen took the chair on Devin's other side.

"I'm okay," Addie said. "Tell us the rest."

He worried that she really ought to eat something. "Maybe you should have some soda crackers or something?"

"James, just tell us what happened."

He speared his fingers through his hair. "What can I say? I tried."

She actually bumped him with her shoulder, a reassuring little nudge that somehow made him feel better about everything. And then she said, "I know you tried. We all do. We also know PawPaw. He has a sort of fixation with situations like this. He lost our grandma June when our mother was just five."

Carmen said, "And our mom, well, she just seemed born to heartbreak. She fell in love with two men and both of them ran off, leaving her behind—and pregnant, both times."

Addie went on, "Both times, our grandpa went looking for those men. Both times, he planned to make sure those fathers-to-be did the right thing. But he never found either of them. Then our mother died having me and Paw-Paw raised us on his own."

"We had a happy childhood," said Carmen softly. "PawPaw saw to that."

Devin said, "You heard how he came after me?"

James nodded. "Levi mentioned something about that yesterday." *While he had me at gunpoint.*

Devin explained, "We'd had a fight, me and Carm, and I'd gone off to Laramie to start my life over again."

Carmen said, "I was too proud to tell him that I was pregnant. I'm ashamed to say I lied to PawPaw and told him that Devin had turned his back on me and the baby."

"I would never do that," said Dev.

"I know you wouldn't," Carmen answered tenderly.

Dev went on. "That time, Levi knew where to look. He got in that ancient green pickup and drove to Laramie. He got the jump on me, kidnapped me at gunpoint, tied me up and drove me back to Colorado."

Carmen chuckled. "Where I promptly went ballistic that my insane old grandpa had kidnapped poor Devin. But then Devin was so glad to see me and I'd missed him so much. I cried and confessed about the baby. And Dev said of course he wanted our baby and he wanted *me*, too." Carmen and Devin shared a long, intimate glance. And Carmen said, "So PawPaw put away his shotgun and Dev and I got married and I moved to Laramie with him."

"And since then they've been busy, having their babies and living happily ever after," said Addie fondly. Then her voice turned harder. "And to this day, PawPaw prides himself on doing what *had to be done*—his words, not mine—so that Carmen and Dev could find the love and happiness they so richly deserve. The way he looks at it, he and his shotgun made everything right."

"Wow," said James. "I guess he figures it worked before, so why not try it again?"

"Exactly." Addie bumped his shoulder again. "Go on. Tell us the rest. What happened when you talked to him just now?"

"It was like talking to a wall."

"I'll bet."

"I tried to make him see that he should listen to you. That it *is* Brandon's baby and not mine, that it *couldn't* be mine, that I never even managed to get you to go out with me, let alone...well, you know."

A soft smile curved her plump lips. A soft smile just for him. He thought how he'd never even gotten a kiss from her, of how much he'd like to have one. Even after all the months she'd kept him at arm's length, even now that he knew she was having Brandon Hall's baby.

There was just something about her. She made the world feel fresh. Brand-new. He'd had more fun taking care of her and helping out with her crazy-ass grandpa over the past twenty-four hours than he'd had in years.

He'd meant what he'd told her. He *liked* helping out— when the one he was helping out was her.

She prompted, "We're listening."

He went ahead and told them. "I knew I wasn't getting through to him, but I kept talking to him, nice and quiet and low, trying to get him to admit he had it all wrong. I kept reminding him that he needed to focus on getting well, that he should listen to his nurses. I said that all of us only want to help him get back on his feet. He mostly just lay there with his eyes shut, now and then opening them and glaring at me like he didn't believe a word I was saying. Finally, I just thought, well, if I could get him to take some liquids, at least, that would be something. I started pushing for that, coaxing him, you know? Telling him to try just a few spoonfuls of broth…"

"And then?"

"Out of nowhere, after several minutes of deathly silence, just as I was about to give up and slink out, he spoke again. He agreed he might have some broth if I would be reasonable."

Carmen made a low, knowing sound in her throat.

Dev said, "Uh-oh."

Addie groaned. "You thought *you* were working *him*." She let out a frustrated cry. "I can't believe you let him do that to you. You should know better."

He couldn't deny it. "Yes, I should. I really should."

"After the way you've worked me in the last twenty-four hours," she scolded, "to get me to let you stay, to coax me to eat, to convince me to keep that suite that is way more than we need and way more than I should ever allow you to—"

James put up a hand. "Do you want to hear the rest of the story?"

She made a humphing sound. "Yes. Go ahead." She glared as hard as Levi had.

He conceded the point. "You're right, okay?"

"Of course I'm right."

"Your granddad puts me to shame when it comes to manipulation. And I have to say, he can be damn charming when he wants to be." Carmen, Addie and Dev all nodded. James frowned. "Where was I? Oh, yeah. So he asked me if I would be reasonable. I said of course I was reasonable. He let me feed him a spoonful of broth, and then another spoonful, and I was feeling like I was really making some progress at last. A couple of the nurses caught my eye and nodded in approval that I was getting nourishment down him. He ate all the broth. I felt like a million bucks and I wanted him to try the Jell-O and…"

Dev clapped him on the shoulder, a gesture of support and understanding.

James said, "I don't know how it happened. Somehow I became totally invested in getting him to eat just a little bit more. And then, quietly, in a ragged but kindly tone of voice, he asked me if I would just try to talk to you, if I would only try to convince you to go ahead and marry me. I don't know. I had that spoonful of Jell-O right up to his mouth and…I agreed. I just said yeah, that I would do that. And he smiled and I smiled and then he took the spoon out of my hand and ate the rest of the Jell-O himself."

There was a silence. Then Carmen sighed.

And Addie said, "That is just not right and you know it's not, James. You've set us back in getting through to him. You realize that, don't you?"

He gave a hopeless shrug. "I'm sorry. I know I blew it."

Carmen hurried to reassure him, "But it's good he ate the broth and the Jell-O." Dev made a low noise of agreement.

Addie shot them each a baleful glance and demanded, "So after he ate the Jell-O, did you at least make it clear that you knew he was playing you? Did you at least say that you shouldn't have agreed to do what he asked, because the baby is not your baby and you and I are *not* getting married?"

He stared at her, at her soft, plump lips and her round cheeks and her golden eyes, which gazed back at him reproachfully. All he wanted to do was reach out, curl his hand around the back of her soft neck and pull her close. She was altogether too independent and she needed someone to lean on.

Those plump lips thinned in annoyance. At him. "James. I have asked you a question."

He made himself answer her. "He ate the Jell-O and he had this pleased gleam in his eyes and… I don't know. I just couldn't stand to disappoint him."

"You are telling me that you didn't even take back your promise to try to convince me to marry you?"

"Yeah," he said bleakly. "That's what I'm telling you."

"Well, that does it," she announced. "You're not getting near him again."

An hour later, Addie went back in to deal with Levi herself. She told him what James hadn't managed to say, what she'd *already* told her grandfather more than once before—that she and James were not getting married and the baby was not James's baby and Levi needed to forget about all that and focus on getting well.

Levi turned his head away. He pretended not to hear her.

And three days later, when he should have been in a regular hospital room and getting close to getting the okay to go home, he was still in CSICU.

Could a man *will* himself not to get better?

Apparently, Levi was doing just that.

He wouldn't eat—or not much, anyway. Just enough to keep the nurses from sticking a feeding tube down his throat. But not really enough to get better.

Instead, he got weaker. He suffered a minor incision-area infection and then another on his leg, where they'd harvested the vein for the bypass grafts. His blood counts refused to return to anything approaching normal. He had shortness of breath and he claimed he was too weak to get up and try to walk a step or two. And when the respiratory therapist worked with him, he put in zero effort to do the exercises she gave him.

He should be improving, the nurses said. But he seemed to have lost the will to get better. They feared pneumonia would be next if he didn't start working to clear his lungs, if he didn't start making an effort to sit up and then walk.

All of them—the nurses, his doctors, Addie, Carmen, Devin and James—they all knew exactly what he was doing. He was betting his own life, scaring them all to death in the interest of getting what he wanted most: Addie and James married.

It was so wrong. Wrong and deluded, dangerous and terrifying. Addie was worried sick and furious, simultaneously and constantly.

Finally, on Monday, a full week after Levi's heart attack and surgery, Addie had James drive her back home. She needed a vehicle and she wanted to check on Red Hill. They set out nice and early, so that James could have the whole day to catch up on his work. He dropped her off at the ranch at a little after eight and headed for the county courthouse. She would take her own pickup back to Denver.

Thanks to Walker and Rory McKellan, everything was in order at the ranch. The horses were all groomed and sleek and healthy. They greeted her with happy chuffing sounds and eagerly munched the carrots she offered them. She couldn't resist saddling her own gray mare, Tildy, and indulging in a long, relaxing ride. Her garden didn't need much care this early in the season, but she spent some time digging in it, getting the rows ready for planting.

At the house, she averted her eyes every time she

walked past the ragged hole in the kitchen floor. She would have to take care of that. But not today.

She went through the mail that had piled up in the past week and separated out the bills she needed to pay, sticking them in her shoulder bag to deal with later. She tried not to think how far behind she was getting on her little side business of making scarecrows on order and for sale on Etsy. Red Hill wasn't a working ranch, really, and it hadn't been since her grandpa was a boy. Over the years, the Kenwrights had sold off the land little by little. Now there were two hundred and fifty acres left, a barn, stables, the large, rambling main house and a foreman's cottage. Addie did whatever she had to do in order to make ends meet. Like boarding horses, growing most of the produce they ate and making cute scarecrows for sale.

She had some new orders, for a bride, groom and baby scarecrow family. For a Raggedy Andy scarecrow and a ballerina, too. Plus, she had shipments of clothes and straw and other supplies that had been delivered in her absence, signed for by Walker or Rory and left in the barn. She checked them over to see what had come.

It was one in the afternoon by then. And being behind on her scarecrows wasn't the priority.

Getting PawPaw to see the light, give up his crazy plan to get her married to James and instead focus on his recovery: that was the priority.

And that was another reason she'd had James bring her home.

Addie went upstairs to the back bedroom she used as her office. In the file cabinet there, she found the paperwork from the sperm bank where Brandon had stored the sperm that had made their baby. She took the file, gathered a few fresh changes of clothes from her bedroom closet and ran back downstairs. Five minutes later, she was out the door and behind the wheel of her trusty pickup, headed back to Denver.

After reluctantly leaving Addie on her own at Red Hill, James drove to the county seat forty miles from Justice Creek. He spent the morning at the courthouse, handling legal matters for various clients. Then he drove back toward Justice Creek, stopping at the Sylvan Inn a few miles outside town, where he joined his half sister, Nell, his half brothers, Garrett and Quinn, and Quinn's wife, Chloe, for lunch.

Together, Garrett and Nell ran Bravo Construction. Quinn, who owned a fitness center in town, had recently started buying houses to flip. His wife, Chloe, an interior designer, would draw up the plans to redesign the dated interiors. Then Garrett and Nell would bring in their crews and start knocking out walls. Once the renovation was complete, Chloe would stage the rooms with furniture and attractive accessories before they put the house up for sale.

James liked all of his siblings and half siblings. They'd had some rough patches growing up, natural resentments created because their father, Franklin Bravo, refused to choose between his wife, Sondra—who gave him four children, James included—and Willow, his mistress, who gave him five more, including Garrett, Quinn and Nell. Over a decade ago, when James's mother died, Frank had promptly married Willow and moved her into the mansion he'd originally built for Sondra. Now Frank was gone, too. Willow lived alone in the house that had once belonged to her rival.

James and his siblings and half siblings were fine with how things had turned out. The years had mellowed everyone. They all tried to show up for the major events: weddings, births, christenings, whatever. James enjoyed having such a big, close-knit family.

He also liked doing business with his brothers and sisters. He'd not only had Bravo Construction build his new house, but put money into Nell and Garrett's company, and he was planning to buy some commercial real estate and then have Chloe, Garrett and Nell fix it up before he put it back on the market. Quinn had expressed an interest in going in with him on that.

It was a good lunch, James thought. Productive. They talked business, kicking around ideas as to which properties might be right for them.

They'd all heard about Levi's heart attack, about how Walker and Rory were looking after the Red Hill livestock and babysitting Addie's dog while Levi was in the hospital. James admitted that he'd been there when the heart attack happened, but he kept the details to himself.

Nell said, "Heard you've been spending a lot of time with the Kenwrights in Denver."

He played it off. "Just helping them out a little when things are tough, that's all. Levi's not recovering as fast he should."

They all expressed their sympathy and offered to pitch in if there was any way they might be needed.

Nell kept after him. "I was at your new house installing the kitchen cabinets a couple of weeks ago, remember?"

He knew exactly where she was going and accepted the inevitable with a shrug. "I remember."

His half sister, who was the beauty of the family with killer curves and a face that brought to mind the sultry singer Lana Del Rey, flipped a hank of thick auburn hair back over her shoulder and reminded him, "Addie stopped by that day."

"She stopped to say hi, that's all."

"I've got eyes, Jamie. You've got a soft spot for Addie Kenwright."

James didn't deny it. Why should he? He did have a soft spot for Addie. And he hoped she was managing all right, whatever she just *had* to do at Red Hill.

He thought of the hole Levi had blown in the kitchen floor and almost asked Garrett and Nell to take care of it. They could get the key from Walker and do the work while the house was empty.

But he knew he'd better discuss it with Addie before he set anything up. She could get testy when he took care of her business without consulting her first. Plus, Nell was bound to ask who'd made that hole and how. He supposed he could tell them what he'd told Sal, the med tech—that Levi had been cleaning his shotgun.

But no. Better not to go there until he'd had a word with Addie about it.

They finished up the meal at a little before two and walked out to the parking lot together, climbing into their separate vehicles, everyone headed back to town. James led the way out of the lot onto the highway, with the others falling in behind him. His plan was to return to the office, where he would catch up with clients, go over his calendar with his secretary and deal with any correspondence that had piled up since he last came in on Friday. Then at five, he would be on his way to Denver again.

It was a nice, sunny day and he drove with the windows down—which meant he smelled the smoke long before he had a clue what might be on fire. Also, he heard the sirens wailing in the distance, to the northeast.

Calder and Bravo, Attorneys-at-Law, had offices on West Central, but he could see the black smoke billowing skyward to the east. His pulse ratcheted up several notches. Damned if it didn't look as though the fire was right there in town.

So he went east on Central, toward the smoke and the sirens. A glance in his rearview mirror showed him that Quinn and Chloe, Garrett and Nell had made the same choice.

Four long blocks later, past most of the shops and businesses that lined Central Street, he saw that the building his sister Elise owned jointly with her best friend, Tracy Winham, was on fire.

The gorgeous old brick structure had three shops on the bottom floor: a jewelry store, a gift shop and Bravo Catering, which Elise and Tracy owned and ran. Tracy and Elise also each had a large apartment on the upper two floors.

Or they used to. Judging by the extent of the fire, the building would end up a complete loss.

The firefighters were on it, though, hoses rolled out, dousing the blaze that had engulfed all three floors. Flames licked out of every window and the smoke, thick and black, turned the blue sky murky gray.

He spotted Elise and Tracy on the sidewalk, well away from the fire. They had their arms around each other as they watched both their homes and their business go up in smoke. In the arm that wasn't wrapped tight around her best friend, Elise clutched her big orange cat, Mr. Wiggles.

James's other full sister, Clara, stood with them, as did his other half sister, Jody. He recognized the owner of the jewelry store and the couple who ran the gift shop and dared to hope that everyone had gotten out safely. Plus, he saw neither flames nor smoke coming from the structures to either side. So far at least, they'd kept the fire from spreading to any other buildings.

He drove on past the fire, past the two fire trucks and

the huddled knots of people on the sidewalk. When he spotted an empty space, he eased his pickup in at the curb. He shoved open his door and hit the pavement at a run, headed back to his sisters and Tracy. Garrett, Nell, Quinn and Chloe followed on his heels.

James was half a block from the fire when it happened.

With a sound like the final gasp of some great, dying beast, the roof of the burning building collapsed inward, sending a river of sparks and live ash shooting up toward the afternoon sky.

Chapter Five

At the hospital in Denver, with the file she'd taken from her office nook at Red Hill under her arm, Addie went straight in to see her grandfather.

He opened his eyes when she said his name.

She took his glasses from the table by the bed and gently put them on his pasty, puffy face. And then she showed him the papers that proved she had been artificially inseminated with Brandon Hall's sperm.

"PawPaw, come on," she whispered fervently. "Face the truth, please. For Carm's and my sake. For Dev and your grandkids, for the sake of everyone who loves you so much. Let it go. Move on. Let yourself get well."

She didn't even know she was crying until he reached up a shaking, wrinkled, bruised-up hand with an IV taped to the back of it and, lightly as moth wings, brushed at the tears that trailed down her cheeks. The touch lasted only a second or two. Then his hand plopped to his side and he let out a soft little sigh, as though just that small effort had thoroughly exhausted him.

She pleaded again. "Please, PawPaw. Please don't do this. I'm not my mother all those years ago, sitting around pining for men who did me wrong. I'm not Carm, letting her pride keep her from telling Dev that he was going to be a dad. PawPaw, won't you just open your eyes and see that I'm having this baby because I *want* this baby? I swear on my life, it *is* Brandon's baby. I got pregnant on purpose and I don't need a man to make things right for me. Things *are* right. Or they would be, if you would only stop this craziness and start trying to get well…" She let her voice trail off and waited for him to say something, *anything*.

But he gave her only silence.

She tried again. "And as for James, you just don't get it. It's not what you think. He's a good guy, that's all. He's a…a friend, you know? He's just trying to help out. I swear to you I've never even kissed that man, let alone *slept* with him. He really, truly is not the dad and my baby is not his problem."

Levi spoke then, his wrinkled lips moving, his stale breath coming out in a rattling little puff.

Hope rising that maybe, just maybe, she'd finally gotten through to him, she leaned closer. "What, PawPaw? Tell me, please. What?"

And he spoke again, just loud enough, finally, that she could make out the words. "Marry James. I'll get well."

Addie gasped in hurt and outrage. "I can't believe you're doing this. Risking your own life to try to force me to do something that is completely my own business, something you have no say in whatsoever. You… you need to stop this ridiculousness right this minute. I…I can't… I don't…" God. She'd run out of words. She sucked in a hard breath and demanded, "What is the *matter* with you? Have you heard a single thing I said to you just now?"

"I heard you. All of it." The words came out raspy and ragged, as if all of him were dry inside, as if he were nothing but a bunch of sticks and brown, crumpled leaves rubbing together in a cold, uncaring wind. And then he said it again. "Marry James."

That did it. She straightened, whirled on her heel and got out fast. If she hadn't, she would have vomited right there on the floor by her dying grandpa's bed.

Carm took one look at her and grabbed her arm. "How long since you ate something?"

"Don't talk to me about eating. I am never going to eat again."

"Oh, great. Turning suicidal, just like PawPaw. And remember, you'll be starving yourself *and* your innocent child."

"Sometimes he makes me just want to scream. Scream and scream and never stop."

Carm locked eyes with Dev. "We're going to the cafeteria."

Dev nodded. "Keep your phone close. I'll call if they need you up here."

Carm wrapped an arm around Addie's shoulders. "This way. Don't argue."

By the time they got down to the basement, Addie no longer felt as if the top of her head was about to blow off from all the fury spinning and popping inside her. Her stomach had settled marginally. And she did know that she needed to eat. She took a tray and got in line behind Carmen.

Once they'd paid the cashier, they got a table by the row

of narrow windows that looked out on a pretty, landscaped walkway where, owing to the cafeteria being mostly underground, the view was of the bottom halves of well-trimmed bushes and people's legs going by.

Carm waited for her to eat a few crackers and sip up a couple of spoonfuls of vegetable soup before asking, "Okay, what was that about?"

Addie had set the file folder on the empty chair beside her. She passed it to Carmen. "I showed him proof that the baby is Brandon's."

Carmen gave the papers inside a quick glance and handed them back. "Didn't help, huh?"

"He actually said right out loud to me that if I married James, he would get well."

Carmen dropped the French fry she'd been about to put in her mouth. "Get outta Dodge."

"God's truth. He did."

"Incredible. I mean, we all knew that was what he was doing."

"Right. But at least until now, we could tell ourselves it wasn't a conscious choice, that he was just so depressed over the failure of his wrong and completely insane shotgun wedding plans, he couldn't focus on getting better."

"But now we know it's much worse." Carmen picked up a triangle of club sandwich, ate a bite and chewed slowly. When she swallowed, she said, "I don't even want to say it out loud."

"Not saying it won't make it any less true."

So her sister went ahead and said it. "He's doing this to himself, risking his own life on purpose."

"Carm. What am I going to do?"

Carmen set the sandwich down and drank a little cranberry juice. "Don't make me tell you. Please."

Addie whispered, "I really think he might not make it if I don't do what he wants."

Carmen whispered back, "At this point, honey, he might not make it anyway."

"Oh, dear God." Addie felt the tears clogging her throat again. "No wonder all I want to do lately is cry and throw up."

Carm reached across the table. Addie met her halfway. They clutched hands and stared into each other's eyes.

Finally, Carm gulped and said what Addie couldn't stop herself from thinking. "I know James would do it if you asked him to."

Addie shut her eyes and drew a slow, steadying breath. "It's just...you know, so wrong to put that on him. He's a good guy and he's been nothing but wonderful about all this. PawPaw knocked him out cold, dragged him to Red Hill, tied him to a chair and threatened him with the business end of his Mossberg Maverick 88. And yet here he is, right beside us, helping out in any way he can, sticking by us through everything. I don't get it."

"Oh, yeah, you do. He's not only a great guy. He's wild for you, Addie Anne."

Addie's throat clutched and her cheeks grew warm. "Oh, you don't know that."

"Yeah. I do. And you want *him*, too. You *could* look at it as taking a chance on love for once."

"I *have* taken chances on love. None of them ended well."

"You took chances on the wrong guys. Look at me and Dev. Things do work out between men and women, you know?"

"Can we not get all down in the weeds about love and romance right now, please?"

"You need to talk about this with James. When's he coming back?"

"I don't know. After he's done at his office, I guess." She cast a desperate, pleading glance at the ceiling. "Dear sweet Lord, I cannot ask such a thing of him."

"Yeah, you can. And you'd better do it as soon as possible. The longer you put it off, the harder it's going to be for PawPaw to pull himself back from the brink of death."

Once they'd eaten, they went back upstairs, where Devin had no news.

Carm took the situation in hand. "Go to the hotel. Try to get a little rest. And call James. Tell him you're in the suite and you want him to meet you there. That'll give you two some privacy for the big discussion."

Addie looked to Dev, who had no idea yet what they were talking about. But Dev was a wonderfully well-trained husband. He just gave her an encouraging smile and went back to playing World of Warcraft on his phone. "The big discussion?" she scoffed. "Carm, I didn't say I would do it. I don't know if I *can* do it."

Carm just looked at her. It was all she had to do. Addie knew what her sister was thinking: *What choice have you got?*

Addie autodialed James as she walked into the suite.

He didn't answer. It was almost four by then and she assumed he must be busy at the office. She left a short message asking him to call her back.

And then she filled up the jetted tub in the luxurious bathroom off the bedroom she and James were sharing— meaning, really, that they took turns crashing in it. She took a long bath, keeping the phone close so she could snatch it right up when he called her back.

But half an hour later, he hadn't called and her skin had started feeling pruney. She got out, toweled off and slathered on the lotion. Once she was dressed again, she debated giving him another call.

But somehow that seemed wrong and way too needy—which, to be brutally honest, was exactly how things stood. She needed him to marry her, and that was all wrong.

Plus, what about her pride?

She knew the answer. Her pride had to go. She was headed straight for the pride-free zone, about to beg a man to marry her in order to keep her pigheaded, self-destructive grandfather from killing himself.

She called James again. Again, there was no answer. She left another message. "Sorry to bother you, really. But if you could just call me as soon as you get this? Please, James. I...need to talk to you." She hung up feeling like the wimpiest, most pitiful creature the world had ever known.

James stayed right there on the street with the family as Elise's building continued to burn.

Once his sister's former home and place of business was nothing more than a soggy, smoking pile of charred bricks, Elise, Tracy and the other shop owners were interviewed by the deputy fire marshal. The gift shop owners confessed that they kept a hot plate in the back of the store. One of them might have left it on by accident. And then they'd both stepped out to run an errand, leaving the shop empty until the flames had already taken hold. Also, when the deputy marshal leaned on them a little, the couple admitted that they'd taken the batteries out of the smoke alarms in the shop because they kept going off whenever anyone wanted to enjoy a smoke.

Elise, already at her wit's end after losing everything but the shirt on her back, burst into tears when she learned all that. She clung to Tracy and to her increasingly agitated cat.

James represented Elise and Tracy. He'd helped them work out the lease, which clearly stated that there was no smoking in the building. Not to mention, Colorado was a smoke-free state. If your business was open to the public, you weren't allowed to smoke in it. As to the fire alarms, it was illegal to disable them. James could see a lawsuit in the works. That was never fun—not for the plaintiff *or* the defendant.

Once the interviews with the deputy marshal were over, Clara asked everyone to come to her house a couple of blocks away. James went along in case there might be some way he could help out. Everyone was worried about Tracy. She'd lost both her parents in a fire. She seemed practically catatonic after living through another disastrous blaze. Elise kept her close and Tracy clung to her.

At Clara's house, Elise finally let go of her big orange cat. Mr. Wiggles promptly took off down the front hall and detoured into the first room with an open door, the master bedroom.

Clara waved a hand. "It's all right. Poor guy needs a little time to himself after all the excitement. He'll probably just hide under the bed, and that's fine with me."

Clara and her housekeeper and babysitter, Mrs. Scruggs, got to work making coffee and scouring the cupboards for snacks to share. Jody and Nell hovered close to Elise and Tracy, ready to get them whatever they needed.

James volunteered to call Elise and Tracy's insurance agent for them, but when he reached for his phone, it wasn't in his pocket. He must have left it in the truck.

Clara told him to use the house phone, which he did. The agent, Bob Karnes, said he'd be right over.

Bob was as good as his word. He showed up half an hour later, got the information he needed to get started on the claim and promised Elise and Tracy he would speed up the process as much as he possibly could.

When Bob left, it was a quarter of five. James couldn't help wondering how things were going in Denver. Addie must be back at the hospital by now. He was getting antsy to check in on Levi's condition, see how Addie was doing and make sure she took some time to eat.

But he knew she got tired of him hovering over her. He told himself nothing that important was going to happen in the next few hours. He'd see Addie and check on Levi's progress as soon as he could get back to Denver.

And right now he had more to do in Justice Creek.

He got Clara aside and gave her the keys to his condo in town. "Give these to Elise when they start trying to decide where to go tonight," he said. "She and Tracy and the cat can have it for as long as they need a place. I'm spending my nights in Denver for the next several days, at least. And my new house is almost ready anyway."

Clara hugged him. "You're the best big brother we ever had."

He grunted and tipped his head toward their brother Darius, who'd just shown up a short time before to see if there was anything he could do to help. "You mean, other than Dare," he teased.

Clara nodded. "Right. You're *both* the best."

He kissed her cheek, went over and gave Elise and Tracy each a last hug and then left for his office. When he got in the quad cab, he didn't see his phone in the console where he usually left it. Had he gone and lost the damn thing? That would be a pain in the ass. It was brand-new, had all the bells and whistles, a boatload of memory, and had cost a lot more than any sane man should pay for a phone.

He went to his office and worked for an hour and a half, eating takeout his secretary, Louise, had ordered for him as he plowed through correspondence, dealing only with the issues that couldn't wait another day. He almost called Addie before he left the building but decided to just get on the road instead.

He was halfway to Denver and it was just after eight when he heard his phone ringing. The sound was coming from under the seat, where it must have fallen at some point during the day. He was on the interstate by then. But he had his GPS connected to the phone for hands-free calling. The earpiece was right there in the cup holder, so he stuck it in his ear and turned on the GPS.

Nothing. At some point, he'd probably switched off the phone's Bluetooth connection. Technology. Never worked when you needed it. There was nowhere safe to pull over, so he just kept driving. But whoever had called left a message, because the phone buzzed at intervals to let him know he had voice mail.

As the intermittent buzzing kept happening, he remembered that he'd heard it before and tuned it out, what with thinking about Elise and Tracy, wondering how Addie was managing, and trying to figure out what he absolutely had to deal with before he could head for Denver again.

Now the buzzing worried the hell out of him. Was Levi okay? Did Elise need something at the condo?

Finally, he couldn't take it anymore. He turned off at the next exit, pulled into a convenience store parking lot and felt under the seat until he finally had the phone. There were four calls from Addie. There was also a text from her asking him to call her as soon as possible. Addie never texted. Her phone was ancient and texting with it took forever. And he had voice mail waiting. She must have left voice messages, too.

Four calls, voice mail and a text. That couldn't be good. He autodialed her.

She answered on the first ring, which freaked him out in itself. Addie never had her phone just waiting in her hand. Not unless there was some kind of emergency going on. "James?" she asked, too softly, then louder and a little bit frantic. "James?"

He couldn't explain himself fast enough. "I'm sorry. It's been an insane day. I had no idea you'd been calling. I lost track of my phone. It was under the seat and I…" Damn. He was babbling like a fool. "Addie, what's happened? Is Levi…?"

"He's okay," she said. "I mean, you know, not good, but still, um, with us."

"What is it? What can I do?"

"Oh, James…" A tiny, muffled sniffle.

"Addie, are you crying?"

Another barely audible sniff. "No. No, of course not. I just thought…"

"You thought what?" He tried to keep his voice even and gentle, in spite of the fact that she was freaking him out.

She sniffed again. "It doesn't matter."

"Addie, that's not true. You can tell me. I'm listening."

"Fine," she said sharply. "I thought, well, that maybe you were just getting tired of me taking advantage of you. I thought maybe you were pissed off because I kept calling and you wanted me to stop bugging you. I thought—"

"Addie."

"What?"

"I'm sorry I didn't call you. I misplaced my phone and there was a lot going on and I was hurrying to get back to you. And *I* didn't want to bug *you*."

She didn't say anything for several seconds. Then, grudgingly, "You never minded bugging me before."

That made him smile. "Hmm. Good point. I guess I decided to give you a break from me at exactly the wrong time."

"Yes. Well, I guess you did."

"You sound better."

"Better? What are you talking about? I'm perfectly fine."

He couldn't help grinning. "Yep. Almost like your old self, all snap and vinegar."

"Gee, thanks," she said. He just knew she was rolling her eyes. "And where are you now, anyway?"

"At a convenience store about forty-five minutes from the hospital. I finally heard the phone buzzing under the seat, so I stopped and fished it out. Are you at the hospital?"

"No. I'm at the hotel. Would you, um, come straight here to the suite? I really need to talk to you."

This didn't sound good. "Addie, what's going on?"

"Can you just come here, please? Directly here? I'll tell you everything, but I need to do it face-to-face."

"Okay, now you've got me seriously worried."

"James, will you just come to the hotel and *talk* to me, please?"

"Okay." Whatever had gone wrong—and he had a feeling it was pretty bad—he needed to be there to help her with it. "Forty-five minutes, tops, and I'm there. I'll turn on the Bluetooth so if you need me again, I can take it while I'm driving."

"The Bluetooth?" she echoed, as though she had no idea what he was talking about.

"I'm just saying, if you call again, I'll be here. I'll answer."

"Just come straight to the hotel."

"I'm on my way."

He made it in thirty-five minutes, pushing his speed the whole way. Luck was with him and no state trooper pulled him over.

At twenty of nine, he was sticking his key card in the slot. Addie must have heard him at the door. She was waiting in the little entry area, barefoot, wearing a Harley-Davidson T-shirt and plaid pajama bottoms, when he came through the door.

"James." She had her hands against her soft lips, and her eyes were all misty. As though he was the best thing she'd seen all day.

"Addie," he said in a whisper, because it felt so damn good to have her looking at him like that.

And then she ran to him, as if he were her guy, as though all she wanted was to feel his arms around her. He grabbed on tight, picked her up and swung her around. Damn, she felt good, soft in all the right places, her full breasts against his chest, her hair warm and silky against his cheek, the scent of her so sweet.

When he set her down, she gazed up at him, all round cheeks, plump lips and red-rimmed golden eyes. He wanted to kiss her more than he wanted to draw his next breath.

But before he could swoop down and claim that tempting mouth for the very first time, she grabbed his hand from behind her back, whirled around and pulled him into the living area.

"Did you eat?" she demanded as she pushed him down on the sofa and then sat next to him.

"I did." He wanted her closer. So he dropped his briefcase beside the couch, hooked his arm around her waist and tucked her into his side.

"James!" she groused. But she didn't pull away. On the contrary, she leaned her head on his shoulder with a sigh.

Whatever bad thing had happened, it had made her reach out to him. He could feel downright grateful for that. He pulled her even closer and stroked her thick, soft hair. "The important question is, did *you* eat?"

"I did. I had lunch with Carm at the hospital. And I had room-service dinner."

"Excellent."

She gave a long, slow sigh. "You said your day was crazy...?"

He put a finger under her chin and tipped it up so she would look at him. "Stuff happened, but it's as sorted out as it's going to get for tonight. I'll tell you all about it later."

"No. Please. Tell me now."

"Addie, what is going on?"

"I need time to build up to what I have to say, okay? And I've been sitting here half the afternoon and into the evening thinking of all the ways I've taken advantage of you, all the ways I haven't *appreciated* you. Thinking that you didn't call me back because you were finally fed up with me and that I totally understood why you would feel that way."

"You're beating yourself up for nothing. You know that, right? You've got it all wrong and I already told you why I didn't call you back."

"I know. But I think it's time I started appreciating you more."

He suppressed a chuckle. "Okay. If you just *have* to."

"I do, as a matter of fact," she replied with great dignity. "And part of appreciating you is listening to how *your* day went. So just tell me what happened in Justice Creek, please."

"You really want to hear about it?" Actually, that she did was kind of gratifying.

"I do. Yes."

So he gave in and told her about the fire. "The building's a total loss," he added at the end. "Elise and Tracy will be staying at my condo for a while."

"Your poor sister. And poor Tracy…"

"Nobody died and they have insurance. Elise even got her cat out safely. It could have been worse."

"Yeah. But to lose your home, all your personal belongings *and* your business on the same day. That's gotta hurt."

"They'll be okay. We'll all pitch in to make sure of that—and now it's your turn. Tell me whatever it is that's so hard to say."

"I don't know how to…" She ran out of steam before she even got going. Her big eyes filled with tears again. "Crap." She pulled free of his arms and dashed the moisture away. "I am not going to cry anymore. I'm not, and that's final."

He wanted to grab her close again, to demand that she tell him right now what had her so upset. But he did neither. He just waited, let her find her own way to it.

And finally, she said, "I thought that if I showed Paw-Paw the documents that proved I really did have intra-uterine insemination with Brandon's sperm, he might finally see the light and admit that Brandon's the baby's dad. So when I was at the ranch, I got the paperwork they gave me at the sperm bank and the bill from the doctor I used. Then when I got back to the hospital, I took them in to PawPaw."

"Did it work?"

She threw up both hands. "Are you kidding? He's made up his mind and no mere facts are going to change it for him."

"I have to say I'm not really surprised."

She hummed low in her throat. "Yeah, well. It was a shot. And the way he blew me off wasn't the worst of it. James, he looks so horrible. I worry he's not going to make it. They're all worried—the nurses, the doctors, Carm and Dev. Every day, he gets weaker. He simply refuses to get well. And today, he told me… He whispered to me…"

James took her hand. She didn't attempt to pull away when he twined his fingers with her smaller ones. "Go on."

And at last, she got down to it. "He said, and I quote, 'Marry James. I'll get well.'" With a soft cry, she yanked her fingers free of his grip and raked them back through her tumbled hair. "I mean, I know it might be too late anyway. He looks *really* bad. It scares me that even if he tries, it's not going to do any good. But I…"

He couldn't stand to watch her suffer as she danced around the real question. "Addie."

"Lord in heaven." She sagged against him and he wrapped his arms around her again. "You know what I'm leading up to here, right?" She whispered the question.

He felt the warmth of her breath against his shoulder and he gathered her just a little bit closer. "I do. And Levi is one tough old bird. I'm thinking if he says he'll get well, there's a better than fifty-fifty chance he can make that happen."

"Still, he could die anyway."

"I don't think he will. But if I'm wrong, he would die believing that he'd done everything he could to see you cared for and protected."

"We both know that's just deluded."

"Yeah, well. Deluded or not, if we got married, he would still die happy."

"It feels so wrong to ask this of you."

"Hey." He waited until she tipped her head up and looked at him. "You haven't even asked yet and I'm already saying yes. Let's get married, Addie. Let's do it right away."

"I just keep thinking about what you said that night you told me about your ex-wife. You never planned to get married again."

"I also said that I was slowly realizing that never is a long, long time."

"Still…" She shook her head. "I hate doing this to you."

"You're not *doing* anything to me. Once, I planned never to get married again. But plans change and I'm going to get married *now*. To you. If you'll have me."

Her soft mouth trembled. "Yes, I will. Definitely. And thank you." She said it prayerfully.

"You're welcome." Trying to lighten the heavy mood, he teased, "Wait a minute. Was I too easy? Do you think I should probably be playing at least a little hard to get?"

"Oh, you…" She fake-punched him in the side and then cuddled back in close once more. "Just until he's better. And then we can, you know, get an annulment."

"However you want it." He rubbed his chin across the crown of her head.

She pulled away. He let her go reluctantly and she retreated to her side of the couch. "I've been thinking about it all afternoon," she said, "about how it would go if you agreed. If he does start recovering, the marriage will have to last for a couple of months—six weeks at the least. He needs time to get well enough that he can't just give up again and start fading away as soon as he finds out we called it off."

"Two months. It's a deal."

"We would have to live together and share a room for that time. I mean, he has to believe that it's the real thing, that we're really trying to make it work. When they let him out of the hospital, I would want you to move in with me at Red Hill. He'll want to be there. And I'll want to be with him."

"I get that. Living at Red Hill for two months is fine with me."

She made a sound midway between a chuckle and a sob. "I kind of think we're crazy to do this."

He didn't. "It's not the least crazy to be doing whatever you have to do to keep an old man you love alive."

She watched him so solemnly. "That's fine for me. He raised Carm and me on his own and he seemed to love doing it. I have a thousand precious, golden memories, all made because of him. Him rocking me, singing 'Down in the Valley' off-key to comfort me, when I was really small and had the flu. Him pushing me on the tire swing out behind the house. Teaching me to ride. Teaching me to drive…

"He gave us a happy childhood, James. I owe him everything. I can't stand for him to die when it's really not his time. I'm so angry at him now. I need him to live for years and years more so I can have time to forgive him for every wrong choice he's made since he conked you on the head a week ago."

"As I said, you love him. And I understand why you love him. Makes complete sense to me."

She chewed nervously on that soft lower lip of hers. "But *you*, on the other hand…"

"Hey, come on. I actually like Levi. And if this will

allow him to focus on getting well, I'm happy to do it." She still gazed at him with doubting eyes. He chided, "Look at yourself. Trying to talk me out of what I've already agreed to do."

She thought about that, tipping her head to the side, her thick, wavy hair tumbling down her arm, shining in the lamplight. "That wouldn't be so smart, would it?"

He shook his head slowly. "Let it be, Addie. We're doing it. We'll get the license first thing tomorrow, and then we'll go tell Levi that if he wants us married, we damn well expect him to stop all this idiocy and live." He didn't like the tortured expression on her face. "You still look worried."

"He's just so…weak, you know?"

"Damn it, Addie. Are you saying you don't think he'll last until tomorrow?"

She shuddered. "No. No, of course not. I called Carm an hour ago. She said there was no change."

He made the decision for her then. "Put some clothes on. We'll go and tell him right now."

"It's late…"

"In this case, Addie, I'm sure the nurses will let us in to see him."

Chapter Six

Twenty minutes later, Addie stood by Levi's bed in CSICU, with James at her side. The night staff had accepted their promise to keep things quiet and a nurse had pulled the privacy curtain shut around them—for their sake and for the sake of the other patients in the unit. The machines that kept track of her grandfather's slow slide toward a too-early end whooshed and beeped very softly around them and the green light from the heart monitor cast a cold glow across the bed.

Levi seemed to be sleeping.

But he opened his eyes when she bent close to kiss his forehead and smooth his dry white hair. "PawPaw," she whispered. As his eyes widened, she stood to her height and reached for James's hand.

His fingers closed around hers, warm and strong. So steady.

Levi blinked several times in rapid succession. The

sounds from the heart monitor sped up—but thankfully not enough to trigger an alarm.

James spoke then. "We came to tell you that Addie and I are getting married."

Addie said, "Tomorrow, we'll get the license."

Her grandfather shut his eyes. A slow sigh escaped him. "Good."

Addie wanted to grab on to him and hold him so he could never, ever slip away from her. She also wanted to shake him and shout at him for being such a stubborn and totally misguided old fool. But she did none of those things. She said, "As soon as you're moved to a regular room, we'll arrange for a pastor and get married right there."

"In my room?" A raspy, thin whisper.

"Yes. As soon as you're well enough to leave ICU."

He let out a dry, crackling sound. It took her a moment to realize it was a chuckle. "Namin' your terms, are you, Addie Anne?"

The truth was, if he didn't improve, they'd ask the nurses if they could get married right here in CSICU. It was all a big bluff. She and James had already agreed that her grandfather was going to get what he wanted. Even if it turned out to be nothing more than the answer to a dying man's last wish—or, in Levi's case, his last demand.

She said, "I am making you a promise, PawPaw. James and I *are* getting married. In your hospital room, as soon as you're out of CSICU."

Carm and Dev jumped to their feet when Addie and James came through the double doors.

Carm asked, "Well?"

"It's done," said Addie. "We told him. And I swear, he almost seems better already."

"Oh, I hope so." Carm grabbed her and hugged her. Then she took her by the shoulders and held her a little away. "I think we all need to go to the hotel and try to get some rest. I'll ask one of the nurses to call if there's any change."

Nobody argued. They were all beat. It was only a block to the hotel, and all three of their vehicles were in the hotel lot, so they walked. Outside, it was snowing. A springtime snow, light and wet, the kind that would be gone without a trace come morning. They wrapped their winter jackets tighter around them and hustled along at a brisk pace.

In the suite, Carm and Dev said good-night and went straight to their room.

James started to offer, "I can take the—"

"Don't even go there," she said wearily. "We're getting married, remember?"

"I just didn't want you to think I was taking advantage of you." He said it lightly, but she knew that he meant it.

She led the way to the bedroom and waited in the open doorway, shaking her head at him. "You're such a gentleman, James."

He crossed the room and dropped to the end of the bed. "A gentleman, huh? That sounds really boring."

"It's not." She shut the door and sagged back against it. "Not in the least."

He arched a thick eyebrow. "Which side do you want?"

Easy. "The one closer to the bathroom?"

"You got it." He crossed one foot over his knee and tugged off a boot. "Put on your pajamas. Let's get some sleep."

"Yes, dear." She dragged herself upright, grabbed the

Harley T-shirt and flannel jammie bottoms off the bedside chair and headed for the bathroom to change.

When she came back out, he took his turn, emerging in a pair of track pants and a dark blue T-shirt, brushing past her on the way to his side of the bed, trailing the minty scent of toothpaste.

They slid in under the covers and reached out simultaneously to turn off their bedside lamps.

"Good night, Addie."

"Night, James." She turned over on her side, closed her eyes and dropped off to sleep in an instant.

James woke to daylight, spooning Addie. And sporting wood. She smelled so good and felt so soft…

He could so easily get ideas.

Okay. He *had* ideas. Always had when it came to her. From that first day he met her, almost a year ago now, when he'd stood on the exact spot where he planned to build his dream house and she appeared in the distance on a gray mare. He'd watched her ride closer, liking what he saw. When she'd reached him, he'd introduced himself and asked her if she'd like a tour of his new house.

"What house?" She'd given him a look that was part wariness and part willingness to play his game.

"You're in the living room, you and your horse."

She swung down off the mare. He'd moved to help her, but she didn't need a man's help to dismount. Her booted feet were already on solid ground. "So it's an invisible house."

"It is now, but not for long."

She'd laughed at that. And then she'd listened intently, her hat down her back and her hair gleaming red-gold under the bright morning sun, as he showed her where each room would be.

In his arms now, she sighed but didn't stir. Was she still asleep? How awkward would it be if she woke up with him wrapped all around her?

He was seriously tempted to find out.

But then he thought about the day ahead of them, getting a license so they could proceed with their shotgun wedding. They were getting married to keep her crazy grandpa alive. Thinking about that kind of ruined the mood.

Very carefully, he pulled his arm from the sweet inward curve of her waist and eased himself back so their bodies were no longer touching.

Addie lay very still, her eyes closed, letting James think she was still sleeping as he slid away and out of the bed. He tiptoed around the end of it and she heard him go into the bathroom and slowly, quietly shut the door.

It had felt good. Right. To wake up with his body pressed to hers. As though that was how it *should* be, the two of them waking up together in the same bed.

Addie groaned, grabbed her pillow out from under her head and plunked it down on top of her face. They were going to spend the next two months or so in the same bed.

And she really needed not to be thinking how amazing it might be to simply let nature take its course.

But already she *was* thinking it.

She put her hand on her flat belly, thought about her tiny little tadpole of a baby swimming around in there. Having a baby without having any of the fun that *made* babies. How fair was that?

She groaned again, pressed the pillow down harder and told herself that no way was she planning to try to seduce James.

And that made her yank the pillow away and plunk

it down on top of the covers and press her hand to her mouth to keep from laughing out loud. She was totally losing it. All the stress and the worry of the past eight days had wrung the sanity clean out of her.

Because, dang it, if she was going to be married to a good, helpful, thoughtful, terrific and very hunky guy, well, why *shouldn't* she get all the benefits of being married to said guy? Even if the whole thing lasted for only eight weeks.

A marriage was a marriage, no matter how short.

James might be a total gentleman, but she really didn't think he'd take all that much seducing. They liked each other, had from the first. They *wanted* each other, even if she had spent the past several months trying to protect herself from the danger of falling for him and eventually finding out—as she always had before—that she'd fallen a lot harder and deeper than he had. She'd tried really hard to pretend she didn't feel the pull.

In the bathroom, she heard the shower start up. "Not going to do that," she said quietly to the ceiling. "Not going to make this situation any more complicated than it already is."

She frowned at the sound of her own voice. Did she sound the least convincing?

No, she did not.

James came out of the bathroom showered, shaved and fully dressed. Addie grabbed her clothes and traded places with him. When she came out, she found him on the couch in the living room, his laptop open on the coffee table in front of him.

He glanced up with a quick smile that did lovely things to all the most feminine parts of her. "I ordered room service. Should be here in fifteen minutes or so. Hope you can get some eggs down."

She realized she was starving. Strangely, when he was around, morning sickness tended to be less of a problem for her. "Eggs sound great." She glanced over and saw that the door to Carm and Dev's room stood open.

James caught the direction of her gaze. "They went back to the hospital."

Her heart rate spiked. "Is PawPaw okay?"

"Relax. There's no emergency. I told your sister we were getting the license first thing. She said that they would hold down the fort at the hospital while we took care of that. She promised to call you right away if there's anything you need to know about Levi."

"Sounds good."

He patted the sofa cushion. "Let me show you what I've found out."

She went and sat beside him. He smelled of soap and aftershave and she wanted to lean against him and have him wrap his arm around her. But then she saw what he'd pulled up on the laptop screen, and her stomach got a knot in it. "A marriage license form?"

"Colorado makes it easy. No blood tests. All you need is valid identification. We can go to the nearest clerk recorder's office—that's in Littleton, less than ten miles from here—and get the license on the spot. And we can make the process even faster if we fill out this form online before we go. Then we go to Littleton, we each produce ID, they bring up our completed form and the license is ours."

They were back at the hospital well before noon.

Addie ran to her sister. "How is he?"

"You won't believe this."

Her stomach turned over. "Oh, God. What now?"

Carm grabbed her and hugged her. "Hey. It's *good* news. He's sitting up. The nurses say he ate broth, a few diced, canned pears and a little bit of toast. He also participated fully for the first time in the session with the respiratory therapist. And he's asked that you and James go right in when you get here with the marriage license."

Levi was sitting up, wide-awake, when they went in. "Let me see it."

Addie longed to roll it into a tube and bop him on his obstinate head with it. But James handed it over.

Levi peered at it as though searching for flaws. But when he lifted his gaze to them, the blue eyes flashed with triumph. "Looks official to me. I'll be in a regular room by tomorrow—Thursday at the latest. Just see if I'm not. And Patty over there..." He gestured toward a nurse at the central nurses' station. She gave him a wink and a big smile. "Patty says they have pastors and priests on call to minister to the critically ill. She says it should be no problem getting a pastor to perform the ceremony in my regular room as soon as I get there."

"We looked into it already," Addie said defiantly. "In Colorado a couple can solemnize their own marriage. We thought we'd do that. It's as legal and binding as if you have a pastor or a judge do it."

"We're havin' none of that," snapped her grandfather. "I want a pastor and that means you're havin' one."

Oh, it was going to take a very long time for her to forgive him for all this. She considered calling him a very bad name. But then she felt James's fingers brushing the back of her hand. She grabbed on tight and said with quiet dignity, "All right, then. A pastor it is."

* * *

Two days later, at nine in the morning on Thursday, eleven days after Levi's heart attack, he was moved at last to his own hospital room. At two that afternoon, Addie and James stood in front of the smiling pastor at Levi's bedside.

James looked so handsome in his beautifully cut dark gray suit with an ice-blue tie. Addie wore a cream-colored lace dress that she and Carmen had bought at Nordstrom the day before. She carried a bouquet of bright Gerbera daisies. Okay, the marriage wouldn't last forever. But she and James had agreed they wanted to look their best when they stood up in front of the pastor.

Devin, who fooled around with photography in his spare time, had gone home Wednesday to check on things in Laramie. He'd brought back one of his digital cameras so he could take pictures of the simple bedside wedding.

Addie tried not to think how sad she would be later, when the two-month marriage was over, to look at the photos of her and James holding hands and repeating their vows. It might bring a tear or two, to see herself clutching her bright daisies, dressed in lace, facing the tall, broad-shouldered man she'd married—but was destined not to keep.

Did it surprise her when James produced a ring? Not really. They hadn't talked about getting one, but he'd spent the day before in Justice Creek, checking on his sister Elise and her friend, and catching up on work. At some point in his busy day, he'd taken time to choose a ring for her.

How like him to think of it—and then to make it happen.

It was a beauty, too. With a double halo of diamonds circling the wonderfully sparkly round central stone and channel-cut stones along the band. He slipped it on first and then the matching wedding band.

She knew he'd spent way too much on it and she almost whispered that he shouldn't have. But it was so beautiful. Why not simply be grateful and enjoy the moment? "Oh, James. And it's a perfect fit. How did you manage that?"

"I asked Carmen your ring size. She took a guess."

"She guessed right. I love it. I do."

The pastor cleared his throat.

Addie giggled. "Oh. Sorry. Carry on."

With a solemn nod, the minister instructed, "James Bravo, you may kiss your bride."

Addie was already looking up into his dark-fringed blue eyes, already feeling that she'd pretty much hit the jackpot as far as temporary husbands went.

And then James slowly smiled at her and she realized that it was actually happening: they were about to share their first kiss.

She stuck out her daisy bouquet and Carm took the hint and whipped it free of her hand.

James said her name, "Addie," softly, in that wonderful smooth, deep voice of his that sent little thrills of excitement pulsing all through her.

She said, "James," low and sweet, just for him. And she thought of the past three nights, of the two of them together in the hotel room bed. Of waking up each morning cuddled up close to him, of one or the other of them gently, reluctantly pulling away...

Okay, maybe it wasn't a *real* marriage. And it would be over as soon as her grandfather was back on his feet.

So what? It was probably as close to a real marriage as she was ever going to get. Her luck really stank when it came to love and forever. She had her mother's special talent for getting it wrong.

But "so what?" to all that, too. She had *this*, didn't she—a certain magic, a certain undeniable attraction to James? She'd spent months denying that attraction. Where had that gotten her?

No place fun, that was for sure.

And now, as he smiled down at her about to kiss her for the very first time, she made her decision.

If James agreed, tonight would be *their* night, a *real* wedding night. When morning came, neither of them would feel that they had to pull away.

So what if they weren't forever? Right now felt wonderful. Right now felt right. And if they *had* to be married for her crazy grandfather's sake, well, why shouldn't she and James enjoy the full range of benefits getting married was supposed to bring?

Addie lifted her face to James. His mouth still curving in that tender, sexy smile, he lowered his dark head to hers.

Chapter Seven

James's lips brushed Addie's, so lightly, a caress and a question both at once. *More?* that kiss seemed to ask.

Longing moved within her. Heat flared across her skin.

Oh, yes, definitely. More.

With a sigh, she put her hands on the fine fabric of his suit, over the strong, hard contours of his deep chest. And then she slid them up to wrap around his neck.

He gathered her closer, his big arms tight around her. He smelled so good and he felt even better. And he tasted like a promise of good things to come.

She parted her lips under his and tasted him more deeply. *Yes*, she thought happily.

Or maybe she'd actually *said* it, maybe she'd kind of breathed the word into his beautiful, oh-so-kissable mouth. Because he lifted away a little and opened his eyes.

And the way that he looked at her...

Definitely. *Tonight.*

They could be as married as they wanted to be when they were alone. It might mess things up for an annulment and they'd end up having to get a divorce.

So what? Divorce or annulment, the end was the end.

He dipped his head to kiss her again and she waited expectantly, her mouth tipped up. But then her grandpa gave a thoroughly annoying raspy little chuckle. Totally wrecked the mood.

James heard that chuckle and arched an eyebrow at her. Reminded all over again of how angry she was at Levi, she pulled a face. He stepped back.

Carm and Dev moved in with hugs and congratulations.

After the pastor left, they all hung around in Levi's room.

James was thoroughly enjoying himself. Why shouldn't he be happy? He'd gotten a first kiss out of Addie. It made him grin to think that he'd had to marry her to get it.

Carmen went out briefly and came back with a cart on which sat a three-tiered wedding cake decked out in frosting flowers. It even had the bride and groom figures at the top beneath a miniature flower-bedecked arch.

Addie laughed. "A cake? You actually went out and ordered a cake?"

"Yes, I did," Carmen replied proudly. "There's a bakery just down the street."

Addie's face betrayed the conflict inside her. James understood. She didn't want to give her grandfather the satisfaction of having a good time at the wedding the old coot had forced on her.

But she *was* having a good time. Her very kissable mouth kept trying to pull into a smile, and that dimple kept tucking itself into her sweet, round left cheek.

In the end, her good nature won out over her anger with Levi. She threw her arms around Carmen and planted a loud kiss on her cheek. "You are the best sister I ever had."

"You bet I am—now get over here, the two of you, and cut this cake. Dev, get the camera ready."

James and Addie mugged for the camera and fed each other the cake and then cut the whole thing into slices so that everyone—the nurses, the clerks, the candy stripers, everyone—could have a slice if they wanted one.

Carmen tried to stop them when they started cutting up the top tier. "You're supposed to freeze that for your first anniversary."

Levi, who was looking healthier by the second and way too pleased with himself, piped up with "Good thinkin'."

Addie ignored her grandfather. Instead, she sidled up close to her sister and whispered something in her ear. James had no trouble guessing what. Something along the lines of *What first anniversary?*

Whatever she said, Carmen pretended to pout. "Just getting into the spirit of things."

"Right." Addie pulled off the little bride and groom and their plastic floral arch, licked the frosting off the base, plunked them down on a paper plate and got busy cutting up the top tier.

The cake was rich and white, with a jam and custard center. Everybody at the nurses' station and up and down the hall wanted some. By the time they were through, there was nothing left but crumbs.

Eventually, at a little after four, the nurses shooed them out so they could look after Levi and make sure he got up and walked around a bit. They all—Addie, Carmen,

Dev and James—decided they were starving, even after all that cake.

So the four of them went out for dinner. James drove. He took them to his favorite steak house downtown, which was just opening its doors for the dinner crowd. James passed the maître d' a fifty and they got a cozy table in a quiet corner. He ordered champagne.

Dev raised a laughing toast. "To the healing power of marriage."

They all laughed at that, even Addie. Marriage—his and Addie's—did seem to be damn good for Levi's health.

Actually, Addie seemed downright happy. James was glad. He'd half expected her to endure their hasty wedding and the aftermath with a grim expression and possibly a couple of quick trips to the ladies' room, because the stress of this whole situation tended to bring on her morning sickness.

But no. She was taking it in stride.

And that kiss—the one that sealed their destined-to-be-short-lived vows, the first kiss he'd ever shared with her?

She'd really gotten into that kiss. The way she'd gazed up at him before and after, well, that look had been something he wouldn't soon forget.

That look had him wondering if tonight was going to be a *real* wedding night.

Was that just wishful thinking?

He hoped not. He'd waited a long time to get Addie in bed—and now that he'd gotten her there the past three nights, well, could anyone blame him for fantasizing about how fine it would be to do more than just sleep with her?

But whatever happened when they were alone together

later, getting married to Addie, even temporarily, was a lot of fun. She might get him even hotter than Vicki did—but that was the only similarity he could find between his first and second wives.

Addie had a big heart. And when she wasn't seething in fury at her grandfather, she was funny and open and easy to be with. She never tried to control him or tell him what to do the way Vicki used to—well, except for the day of Levi's heart attack, when she had been constantly trying to send him on his way.

She really didn't seem to want to get rid of him anymore. He decided to take that as a positive sign.

When they were ready to leave the restaurant, he had to practically wrestle Devin to claim the check. But he pulled rank, being the groom and all. He paid the tab and they returned to the hospital, where they all went in to see Levi one more time that night.

Addie's granddad was cheerful and talkative. He had some color in his cheeks again. James smiled at the sound of that cackling laugh of his. If James's marrying Addie had done that for the old miscreant, it was more than worth it as far as James was concerned.

Levi said that the day had been one of the best of his life. "Because my girls are both married at last, I got two great-grandkids and another on the way. And it looks like I'll live, after all."

Addie got kind of quiet then. James knew, by the way she pressed her lips together and avoided looking at Levi directly, that she remained angry with him for what he'd made her do.

And Levi, being Levi, just couldn't leave it alone. "Addie Anne, stop lookin' like you sucked a giant lemon and give your old PawPaw a hug."

Silence. The old man and the pretty woman in the white lace dress stared each other down.

Carmen cleared her throat. "Go on, Addie. Give him a hug."

Addie made a scoffing noise, but then she did step up closer to Levi's bed, pressed her round cheek to his wrinkled one and then kissed him on the forehead. "I love you, PawPaw," she said in a whisper as grim as her expression.

For once, Levi had sense enough to leave it at that.

At a little after eight, Carmen insisted that the newly-weds should go back to the hotel. "Dev and I will be along eventually—don't wait up, though. I'm not sure how late we'll be."

Devin frowned. "I was kind of thinking we might— Ouch!" He sent Carmen a wounded glance. James couldn't be sure, because he and Addie were on the other side of Levi's bed from Addie's sister and Devin, but it appeared that Carmen had kicked him to get his attention. Devin coughed into his fist and added, "You know what? Forget what I was thinking. You two go ahead."

James waited for Addie to object—and for Levi to make some joking comment that would get Addie angry all over again.

But Addie just said, "Good idea. James, you ready to go?" She held out her hand. James took it happily. How long had he waited for her to reach for his hand?

Too long.

She bent to the bed and gave her grandfather one last kiss.

The old man looked over her bright head and directly at James. "Proud to have you in the family, son." He seemed completely sincere.

James felt a stab of guilt that they weren't giving Levi the marriage he'd bargained for. But really, why feel guilty for disappointing a master manipulator? James tamped down the self-reproach and answered, "Thanks, Levi. I'm a lucky, lucky man."

Addie laughed. It was a carefree sound. James drank it in, loving it, loving that she held his hand as tightly as he held hers. "Let's go." She pulled him through the door and out into the hallway.

It was snowing again, but he'd left the quad cab in the underground hospital lot, so they took it back to the hotel.

In their room, she ushered him ahead, shut and locked the door and followed him over to the side of the turned-back bed. She caught his hand and then gazed up at him, her cheeks flushed the prettiest pink.

He dared to reach out and cradle her face with his free hand. Her scent teased him—flowery, a little tart, wonderfully sweet. "You're a beautiful bride."

She sighed. Her breath smelled like apples, like the cinnamon tea she'd had after dinner. "We shared our first kiss today." She said it softly, almost shyly.

He couldn't help smiling. He rubbed the back of his fingers along the silky side of her neck. That brought another sigh. He was becoming more and more certain that tonight would be a night he would never forget—the kind of night he'd given up on ever having with her. "I knew I would love the taste of your mouth. And I do."

She trembled a little. "I...well, I always told myself that I was never going to kiss you."

"I'm so glad you changed your mind." He traced the line of her thick red-gold hair, where it fell along her plump cheek.

"I don't know. It never seemed safe to kiss you."

"Because I'm such a dangerous guy?" He ran his index

finger down the slope of her pert little nose, loving the way it turned up at the tip. The texture of her skin pleased him immensely, so soft, so smooth, just begging for his touch.

Those amber eyes looked enormous right then. Huge and shining, staring up at him. "You are dangerous to me."

"We should talk about that."

"Maybe someday—and it's not that I haven't wanted to kiss you. I have wanted to. So much. For such a very long time."

"We have a lot of missed kisses to make up for."

She shocked him by agreeing. "We do. And I have a question."

"Shoot."

"There's a tiny white scar." With a finger she brushed the tip of his chin. "Here. How did you get it?"

"School-yard brawl with my half brother Quinn," he said. "We had issues, back then, in the family, what with my father essentially having two wives—my mother, Sondra, and Quinn's mom, Willow."

Addie nodded. "That must have been hard on you— all of you." She didn't ask him to explain any of it, and he wasn't surprised. Pretty much everyone in Justice Creek had heard the old story.

He said, "When we were kids, we resented each other, and we took sides. My mom's kids against Willow's kids."

"Even though what your parents did wasn't their children's fault?"

"We had to get older and wiser to figure that out. In the meantime, when we were kids, sometimes we boys argued with our fists."

"But you all get along now?"

"Yeah, we do. I like my family a lot."

"I'm glad. Family matters."

"It certainly does." He traced the perfect shape of her ear and then caught her earlobe and rubbed it gently between his thumb and forefinger. She wore pearl studs, and the single pearl felt so hard and smooth against his thumb, in contrast to the velvety texture of her skin. He let himself imagine touching her all over, tracing every curve, pressing his lips to her most secret places.

Making her moan for him.

Making her beg.

She started to say something.

He interrupted her. "Kiss me again. Do it right now."

She caught her lower lip between her small, straight teeth. "I want to kiss you. I want to do *more* than kiss you."

"I'm up for that." Oh, yes, he was. Already. Just from the feel of her skin and the look in her eyes and the shy, sexy way she called him dangerous.

"It's just that I...well, I didn't plan ahead." Her cheeks, already flushed, went deep red. "No condoms. And yeah, I'm already pregnant. But babies aren't the only thing that should be considered. I believe in safe sex—I mean, if a person is going to have sex. I just, well, I didn't realize how I would feel now, alone with you, you know? How much I would want us to have a real wedding night, after that wedding kiss, after standing up beside you in front of that pastor, after all of it, everything you've done, James. All the ways you've been about the best guy I've ever known."

Her words made an ache in the center of his chest to match the one growing beneath his fly. He pressed his hand to her cheek. Burning hot with her blush. Beautiful. "I bought some yesterday."

Impossible, but her eyes got even wider. "You did?"

"After I bought the ring, I stopped in at a Walgreens. I didn't really think it would happen. But I knew I'd be an idiot not to be ready if it did."

She actually giggled. "I guess that makes me an idiot."

"No way. How could you plan ahead? You only made up your mind about this today."

"See?" She pointed her finger at the tip of his nose. "That. You are always doing that. Saying just the right thing when you really don't have to."

He caught her pointing finger and kissed the tip of it. "I guess I should just accept my own wonderfulness."

"Yes, you should—and if you bought them, where are they?"

He pressed his lips to the back of her hand. "In my briefcase."

"Go get them."

"You sure you'll be all right if I leave you here alone?"

She leaned up, brushed a kiss against his jaw and whispered, "You should hurry. I'm very impatient."

He swooped to catch her mouth and succeeded, if only briefly. "Don't move."

"I won't. Go."

His soft briefcase was braced against the wall by the door. He went to it, unzipped the center pocket, took out the box and brought it right back to her, dropping it on the nightstand and reaching for her.

She laughed and stepped back. "Not so fast."

"Bossy woman."

A slow, naughty smile. "Take off your jacket."

He did, tossing it onto the bedside chair. "My turn."

She looked at him from under the fringe of dark eyelashes. "We're taking turns?"

"It's only fair. Take off that dress."

Now she fluttered those eyelashes at him. "I might need help with the zipper."

"Turn around."

She did, showing him her back, smoothing her hair out of his way. Stepping right up, he took that zipper down and then couldn't resist pressing his mouth to the sweet bump at the top of her spine, causing her to suck in a sharp breath that proved all over again she was every bit as into this as he was. She pulled her arms free of the snug lace sleeves.

"Don't," he said.

She stopped. "Don't what?"

"I want to see you."

She faced him again. "Like this?" At his nod, she took the dress down to her waist and then wiggled it off over her hips. It dropped around her ankles. She bent and scooped it up.

"Give it to me." She handed it over and he dropped it on top of his jacket.

Now she stood before him in her shoes and white satin bra and lacy panties. And nothing else. Except for her earrings, a thin gold necklace and a lacy blue garter. She must have noted the direction of his gaze, because she pointed at the garter. "Something blue. I bought it when I bought the dress—which makes the dress something new." She touched the delicate gold chain around her neck. "I borrowed this from Carmen. And the pearl earrings are Carm's, too. They're also old. They were my grandmother's."

He reminded himself that they were married only because Levi had forced them into it, that she was having another guy's baby and they'd agreed that they'd be together for only two months. Still, he was an old-fashioned guy at heart. It pleased him no end to think of her finding a way to observe a few wedding traditions.

"It's my turn, James." That adorable dimple tucked itself into her soft cheek.

"Don't rush me." He took his time admiring her, from the top of her strawberry head to the tips of her high-heeled shoes. So curvy and strong. "Perfect in every way."

"Thank you. And at this rate, we'll be getting un-dressed all night long."

That didn't sound like a bad idea to him at all. "What next?" he asked with real enthusiasm.

"Your shoes and socks and tie *and* your shirt."

He didn't argue, just jumped on one foot and then the other, getting rid of his shoes and socks. Off went the tie to join the clothes already on the chair. A minute later, the shirt landed there, too. "Shoes," he instructed.

She took them off and ordered, "Belt and pants."

He got rid of those and remarked with a groan, "Now I'm getting eager."

Her gaze wandered down to the front of his boxer briefs, and her smile brightened the dim corners of the lamp-lit room. "I can see that."

He commanded, "Bra, panties, garter."

"I will be naked," she warned and shook a finger at him.

"Looking forward to that."

Swiftly, with deft, no-nonsense movements that left his mouth dry and his body yearning, she reached be-hind her and undid the bra clasp, slipping the straps off her pretty shoulders and tossing the bit of satin at the chair. Damn. Her breasts were so pretty, round and full, tipped in soft pink the same color as her lips. Had his mouth gone dry a moment ago? No more. Now he was practically drooling. She slid down her panties, taking the garter with them, and kicked both away.

That did it. He couldn't live another second without having his hands on her. "Come here." He reached for her.

She danced back, giggling. "Boxer briefs."

He didn't argue, just eased them over the part of him that was aching to get to her and shoved them off and away. "Come here."

She put her hands to her red cheeks. "Oh, James. You are handsome all over."

"I said, come here."

"And you keep calling *me* bossy." She took off the gold chain and the earrings and set them on the nightstand. "There."

He couldn't wait another second to get his hands on her, so he grabbed for her. That time, she let him catch her. Hauling her close, he pressed his mouth to her temple and breathed in the wonderful, sweet scent of her hair, drank in the feel of her silky skin pressing all along the front of him. Nothing had ever felt so good as Addie naked in his arms.

She wrapped her arms around him, held him as hard and tight as he was holding her. And she whispered, her breath warm against his shoulder, "I don't care what happens, how it all ends up. Because tonight I'm just…so glad. Glad that we're right here, right now, you and me…"

He captured her chin and tipped her face up. Lowering his mouth to hers, he kissed her deeply as he guided her down to the bed.

She went willingly, clinging to his shoulders, her tongue meeting his, wrapping around it, eager and shy at once.

He stroked a hand down the center of her. So much to touch. He could never, ever get enough.

But damned if he wasn't determined to try. He captured one sweet, round breast, teasing it, rubbing the pink nipple between his thumb and forefinger, drinking in her moan as she lifted her body up for him, offering him everything he'd thought never to hold.

He kept on kissing her as his touch strayed lower, into the hollow just under her rib cage, her skin softer than ever there. And down, over her belly all the way to the neatly trimmed dark gold curls at the juncture of her strong thighs.

She cried out when he parted her. He dipped a finger into her slick heat. He drank her cry as he touched her, stroking her, loving the way her body moved for him, the way she lifted into his touch.

He wanted to taste her everywhere. So he let his mouth follow the path his hands had blazed, down and down. Gently, he guided her, lifting one sleek leg and easing under it, until he could settle between her open thighs.

"James?" she asked, a little nervously. "James, are you sure you want to…?"

"Shh," he said. "I do, yes. I do…"

With a sigh, she surrendered.

And he kissed the sweet feminine heart of her. She tasted just right, salty and musky, so slick and so wet. He took his time with her, driving her higher, until she clutched his head and called his name as she went over.

After that, well, yeah, he was eager, hurting even, to plunge into her softness. But some things in life should be done right. This, his first time with Addie?

This fell cleanly into the "do it right" category.

He kissed his way back up her body, turned her to face him and gathered her tightly to him, with both of them on their sides. She reached down between them and wrapped her fingers around him.

"You do that, no telling what will happen," he warned in a growl.

She pressed a sweet, hot kiss to the base of his throat, sticking out her naughty tongue and licking up the sweat that clung to his skin. "I love this, touching you. I've waited way too long to do this."

He groaned in approval—and then couldn't resist razzing her a little. "Why *did* you wait so long?"

"I've had enough man trouble in my life. I was determined not to go there again." She wrapped her fingers tighter around him.

Tight enough she made him groan again. He breathed carefully through his nose and cradled her cheek in his palm. "What do you mean, exactly, by man trouble? You never say."

She tried to look away. "Never mind."

He eased his thumb beneath her chin, holding her sweet face in place, waiting until she looked at him again. Then he said, "Whoever it was, just tell me. I'll bust his face in for you."

She made a disapproving sound. "Really? Seriously? You want to talk about that now?" And then she stroked that hand of hers up and down the length of him, holding on wonderfully tight as she did it.

What were they talking about? He forgot. He forgot everything but her name. "Addie…"

"Shh." She slowed her hand, rubbing, rotating her grip as she caressed him. It was pure agony, but in such a good way.

In the end, he had to grab her wrist and hold her still. "This first time, I want to be with you. I want to be in you…"

She pressed her lips to his throat, to his jaw, and finally she took his mouth, spearing her hot little tongue in, making him groan deep and hard, and then pulling back enough to gaze into his eyes as she continued to stroke him with that determined, clever hand. "However you want it, James, that's how it will be."

"I love it when you pretend to be obedient."

"As long as we're clear that it's only pretend." She kissed him again.

He felt her smile against his mouth and advised, "So, then, in the interest of my not losing it too soon, I think you should maybe let go of me..."

She made a low, purring sort of sound deep in her throat. "Not a chance." And then she gave him a cruel, hard little squeeze that brought another groan up from the deepest part of him. "But I'll be careful not to push you too far."

He gritted his teeth, it felt so good. "You have no idea how close I am to losing it."

"But you won't lose it, will you?"

He never ought to argue with her. It never got him anywhere. With another groan, he reached across her beautiful, naked body and snatched the box off the nightstand. One-handed, he flipped back the lid and whipped out what they needed. "Help."

She took pity on him, letting go of his aching hardness and taking the box from him. She set it back on the nightstand and then took the still-wrapped condom. "Lie back. I've got this."

With a shaky sigh, he rolled to his back.

She unwrapped the condom and carefully rolled it down over him. "There," she said with a pleased little smile.

"Addie." He reached up and clasped her shoulders.

She met his eyes with the softest little smile. "What?"

"Ride me."

For once, she didn't argue, just swung one of those muscled horsewoman's thighs across his hips, lifted herself up onto her knees above him and then reached down to put him right where she wanted him.

"Addie," he whispered, dying a little in the best kind of way. "At last."

She really was something. He'd waited so long for this, to see her like this, bare and open to him, lost in her pleasure. On her knees above him, golden eyes watching him, baby-doll lips parted, her breath coming shallow and fast, she lowered her body down to him, taking him, all of him, in a sweet, perfect glide.

Tight. Hot. Wet.

So exactly what he wanted, so completely right.

"James?" A sweet flush suffused the soft skin above her breasts. With a moan, she came down to him, her body curving over him, settling against his chest, her hair falling forward, brushing his throat, sliding like ribbons of satin along his arms. "Oh, James. Oh, my goodness…"

He gathered her close. Never in his life had he been anywhere sweeter than buried in Addie on their wedding night. "There's no one like you, Addie. No one in the whole world…"

"It's good," she whispered. "James, it's so good with you…"

And then she was kissing him, her mouth wet and open over his, her hair so silky and warm all around him, her body taking him, holding him, owning him, so good and deep.

Making him crazy in the best kind of way.

He groaned her name. She gave his back to him.

And then he slid his hands down and took hold of her fine, round bottom. He surged up into her.

She shouted his name then, out good and loud. And then she was riding him, hard and fast, racing to the finish. He held on and went with it, with her, as he felt her body tightening, reaching...

And then it happened, both of them going still, not even breathing. Until she cried out again—and unraveled around him, her inner muscles contracting, releasing and then clutching him tight once more.

That did it. He couldn't hold out a single second longer.

He rolled, taking her with him, claiming the top position. Another cry escaped her, a softer cry. And yet somehow a wilder one, too.

She lifted her legs and wrapped them around him.

By then, he was gone, lost in her, lost in the searing heat that set the air on fire between them, in the connection they shared that she'd denied for so long.

But not tonight. Tonight she had no denials. Tonight she belonged to him. At last.

James and Addie. Like this.

The way he'd always dreamed they might be.

He buried his face against her throat and gave himself up to her, pushing hard into her, so far gone in her that nothing else existed. There was only Addie, holding him. Addie, whispering naughty, sexy things.

Addie, moaning his name again as the world spun away.

Chapter Eight

"A home nurse?" Levi sucked in a breath of pure out-rage and then groaned because it hurt his incision. Addie could almost feel sorry for him. Except that, as usual, he was being a major pain in the butt. "Don't be ridiculous," he barked. "I don't need a nurse and we don't need to go wasting good money on one—and, son..." He turned to James with another groan of pain. "Do you have to hit every damn bump in the highway? You're killing me here."

"Sorry," James answered mildly. "I'll watch that."

Levi groaned yet again and shifted uncomfortably, pulling on the seat belt to loosen it up a little.

It was exactly a week since Addie had married James. They were on their way home to Red Hill at last—James, Levi and Addie in James's roomy quad cab. Levi had the passenger seat, where they'd thought he'd be the most comfortable, and Addie had taken a seat in back.

Somewhere on the highway not too far behind them, Carmen followed in Addie's old pickup. Dev had returned to Laramie a few days before.

James caught Addie's eye in the rearview mirror. Was that an "I told you so" look he was giving her? It certainly appeared to be. He'd thought they should tell her grandfather about the nurse sooner. She'd vetoed that. Levi wasn't going to like it, no matter when they told him, so she'd decided to do it during the ride home, thus limiting at least the duration of the fit he was bound to pitch over the idea of paying a professional to help with his recovery.

Addie narrowed her eyes at her temporary husband to signal that she had this handled; she knew what she was doing. She told her grandfather, "It's not going to cost us anything. We have the best insurance money can buy, thanks to Brandon—you remember Brandon, PawPaw? My sadly departed best friend and the father of my baby? Brandon wanted us to have really good insurance for the baby's sake and also because when something terrible happens to someone you love, the last thing you need is to be stewing over how to pay for high-quality care."

Levi exchanged a glance with James. They'd been doing that a lot in the past few days, silently communicating their manly thoughts, whatever the heck those were. Sometimes she found it kind of sweet that they got along so well.

Right now she wanted to tell them both to knock it off.

Levi blew right on by her pointed remarks about Brandon and the baby and insisted, "I can take care of myself."

"But a trained nurse can take care of you even better. And that's what you're getting. You're getting the best care."

"You just tell that nurse not to come."

"She's already moved in at Red Hill."

Levi made a sputtering noise followed by more grunts of pain.

Addie said, "Her name is Lola Dorset. She's a retired RN. She will see that you take your meds and eat right. She will supervise your exercises, all of them, strength, cardio *and* breathing. She'll get you out walking but not let you overdo it. She'll be helping you bathe and making sure you take proper care of your incision sites."

"My incision sites are doing just fine, thank you. And no strange woman is going to be giving me baths."

Addie suppressed a sigh. "Strange women—and men—bathed you in the hospital there at first when you refused to start getting well. You weren't complaining about it then. And Lola is only there to help. Whatever you can manage for yourself, fine. But she will be ready to push you when you need it, to offer encouragement, too. She'll be all about you for the next six weeks, at least—with a little help from a relief nurse two days a week and evenings whenever Lola wants time to herself. You need someone who's all about you right now, and we were lucky to get Lola. She only takes a few jobs a year now. And when she chooses to work, she doesn't mind living in. As a matter of fact, James found her for you."

Her grandfather scowled in James's direction and accused, "So you're in on this, too?"

James gave an easy shrug and evaded the question. "Lola looked after my great-aunt Agnes when Agnes had hip surgery two years ago."

Addie added, "Lola is about as good as it gets for home nursing care, PawPaw. You should be grateful that she's going to be looking after you."

"*Grateful* is not the word that comes to mind," grumbled Levi. "*Unnecessary.* That's the word for your precious

Lola. How many ways do I have to say it? We don't need her. You and Carmen can—"

Addie cut him off. "Carm has a life, in case you didn't notice. And she needs to get back to it today. Both she and Dev have used up their family leave. She misses her kids—and she misses her husband, too, now he had to go home and get back to work."

"Humph," her grandfather said. "You and me and James will manage just fine."

"No. No, we will not. James has an office he needs to go to now and then. And I have a mountain of scarecrow orders to catch up on. I also have the horses to look after, not to mention all the chores you won't be doing for a while yet. It's a critical time in your recovery and you need a professional to help you make the most of it. Lola Dorset will be seeing to it that you get exactly what you need."

Silence from the front seat. Apparently, she'd actually managed to overrule all of his objections.

Did she feel like a bully? Oh, well, maybe a little. But sometimes, with her grandfather, bullying was the only way to go.

James caught her eye in the mirror. She scowled at him defiantly. For her sour face, he gave her a wink.

The guy was a prize. No doubt about it. Supportive, smart, funny and kind. Also easy on the eyes and amazing in bed. Every day it got a little harder to remember not to let herself get too attached.

Lola, a trim woman with chin-length silvery hair and excellent posture, was waiting on the front porch when they drove up. Two days ago, when Addie had met her here at the house to give her a set of keys and show her around, the nurse had asked what the family would prefer her to wear. Addie had advised comfortable street clothes. So today, Lola wore new-looking jeans, white running shoes and a long-sleeved Henley shirt.

Addie's dog, Moose, sat at the nurse's feet. Walker McKellan had dropped him off just that morning. The dog ran to greet them, but the nurse stayed where she was.

With a glad cry, Addie shoved open the backseat door. "Moosey boy, I've missed you so much."

The sweet chocolate Lab bounced up on his hind legs with excitement and let out a bark, then remembered his manners and dropped to sitting position. A shudder of pure happiness wiggled through him and he whined for her to get down there and say hi.

Addie jumped from the cab and dropped to a knee. "That's my good boy…" She threw her arms around him, breathed in his dusty doggy smell and let him swipe his wet tongue across her cheek. "We're home," she whispered gratefully into his short brown coat. "Home at last…"

James got out and came around to her. When Moose gave him a whine of greeting, he patted the dog on the head.

Levi pushed open his door. "Ah. It's good to be home." He sounded happy, too, in spite of the recent battle over Lola and whatever pain the ride home had caused him. Addie's heart lifted to hear him sound so cheerful. Then he muttered, "That her?" and tipped his wiry white head in Lola's direction.

Lola must have heard him. She came down the steps. "Yes, Mr. Kenwright. I'm Lola, your nurse." That silvery hair really shone in the sunlight. She gave him a cool smile as she strode confidently toward him.

He already had the seat belt undone and he swung

his legs out. Addie stifled a nervous cry for him to be careful.

James simply stepped into position so that Levi could brace an arm on his shoulder to ease his way down. It was gracefully done, with zero fanfare. Just the way her grandfather liked it. "Thanks, son."

"Anytime." James reached into the cab and pulled out the cane they'd bought him a few days before. "Here you go."

Levi took it with a nod and leaned on it gratefully.

Lola marched right up to him and slipped her hand around his free arm. "Walk me inside, will you? Let me show you how we've set things up."

"Take it slow," he replied, sounding perfectly content— as if he hadn't just given Addie all kinds of grief for hiring the woman. "Some fool doctor cut my chest open two weeks ago and I'm not as spry as I used to be."

Lola laughed. It was an easy, throaty sound. "One step at a time."

Levi actually smiled. "That's the way you do it." Slowly, the two of them started for the house. "You call me Levi," Addie heard him say when they were almost to the steps.

"Levi it is."

James, who was standing right behind Addie, put his big hands on her hips and whispered in her ear, "I told you she was something else."

"Amazing. She's got a real talent with grumpy old men."

"And with bossy old women, too. Have you met my great-aunt Agnes? She can be difficult, to put it mildly, but she took to Lola on sight." He pressed a kiss into her hair.

She started to lean back against him, because then

he would wrap his arms around her and that always felt wonderful. But right then, Carm rolled into the yard and stopped the pickup a few feet from James's quad cab. Reluctantly, Addie suggested, "We should get our suitcases inside so Carm can be on her way back to Laramie."

He made a sound of agreement and let go of her waist. They turned together to get the bags that waited under the camper shell.

He handed her the one that belonged to Levi. "I'll take your suitcase and mine upstairs."

She thought about sharing her bedroom with him for the next several weeks and liked the idea way more than she probably should. It was altogether too much fun playing newlyweds with James. "We're the big room at the front. Turn left at the top of the stairs, left again at the end of that hall and it's the only door on your left. I'll get up there this afternoon and clear you out some drawers and closet space. You can put your stuff away this evening."

He held her gaze, a lovely, intimate look that sent hot little sparks dancing across the surface of her skin. "Sounds like a plan."

Way back in the day, when Levi had married Addie's grandmother June, he'd bumped out walls and added on a master suite for his new bride. The large bedroom, bath and walk-in closet were on the ground floor off the central hall. Now, all these years later, the suite was a godsend for Levi's recovery. He wouldn't be stuck upstairs most of the time, or have to make a temporary bedroom of one of the downstairs living areas.

Addie had given Lola the upstairs bedroom that faced the backyard. It was closest to the stairs. The nurse had brought handheld monitors—a two-way system. Not only could she hear if Levi needed her, but she could communicate with him, find out what he needed without having to run down to his room first.

Also, they'd replaced Levi's old four-poster with a fully adjustable recliner bed that would not only be more comfortable, but would be easier for him to get in and out of, too. When Addie carried his suitcase in there, Lola had him on the bed and was showing him how to work the controller.

"I like this bed," he was saying as he raised himself slowly to a sitting position. "I could get used to this."

"It's a nice one," Lola agreed. "I think you'll be very comfortable."

About then, Levi spotted Addie. "I took a peek in the kitchen. Who fixed the floor?"

Addie set down the suitcase in the corner by the door to deal with later. "James's brother Garrett sent some people over." James had asked her the morning after their wedding if it was all right to hire Garrett to fix the floor—and to install up-to-code grab bars for Levi in the master bath while he was at it. Addie had given the go-ahead. She'd also insisted that she wanted the bill sent to her. So far, that bill had failed to materialize. She made a mental note to remind James that she would pay for both the floor repair and the bath railings, thank you very much.

"Looks good," the old man said cheerfully. "I like the new tile." As though it had been some everyday home improvement project. He gave Lola a distinctly cheeky grin. "I had a little accident cleaning my shotgun."

Lola was sympathetic. "That must have been scary."

Addie couldn't resist grumbling, "You have no idea," as she left them alone.

Back out in front, Moose trailed after her down the

steps. She found the back of the quad cab still open. Only Carmen's suitcase and overnight bag remained inside. They'd already agreed that James would drive Carm into town, where she could pick up a rental car and head for home. Addie closed up the back and turned for the house as James came down the front steps.

"Everything's in," he said. "I like those two dormer windows in your bedroom, with those cozy window seats."

She nodded. "That used to be Carm's room when we were kids. I got it when she married Dev. Hated to see her go—but loved getting her room."

He came closer and guided a few strands of hair out of her eyes. She gazed up at him, thinking how good it felt to be close to him, how great they got along. More than once in the past few days, she almost forgot that by the end of May, they wouldn't be married anymore. "Where's Carm?"

"I think she's saying goodbye to your grandfather." With a sweet brush of his finger, he traced her eyebrows and then the shape of her nose, thrilling her with those simple, silly caresses, and then slid his warm fingers back under her hair to cradle the nape of her neck.

"What are you up to now?" She tried to sound suspicious, but somehow it came out all breathless and hopeful.

"I'm off to work for the rest of the day. Any reason I shouldn't kiss my wife goodbye?"

"No reason at all." She lifted her lips to him and he settled his wonderful mouth over hers.

Time and reality faded off into nothing. There was only the two of them in that hazy, hot, beautiful place they went to whenever they touched.

Oh, she had a mad and crazy crush on him. She kept trying to remember all the reasons they shouldn't get too close, all the ways love and romance never had worked out for her.

But somehow, when he touched her, when he kissed her, whenever he was near, she forgot her bad track record with the male gender, forgot how, after the last time two years ago with Donnie Jacobs, who had sworn that he loved her and wanted forever with her one night and then told her the next night that they were through, she'd finally accepted that romance was just a bad idea for her. She took love way too seriously and she always ended up with her heart cut to ribbons.

She and James should probably talk about that, about how they had to watch themselves, not let things get too intense. They both needed to remember that this wasn't forever.

But then again, just because *she* kept forgetting that this wasn't the real thing, that didn't mean *he* was having any problem keeping his grip on reality.

And please. Did they *really* need to go there, to talk about all the reasons they shouldn't let themselves get carried away?

Why make everything heavy and grim? Why not just enjoy themselves for the time they had together? Too soon, it would be over and she would be big as a house with the baby. And then she'd be a mom, with a newborn to care for. Beautiful, sexy nights like the ones she shared with James right now would be pretty hard to come by.

Why shouldn't they wring every drop of pleasure out of this marriage PawPaw had forced on them? Why not think of it as a fabulous, smokin'-hot fling, and leave it at that?

"What is it with you two? Like a couple of newly-weds," Carmen teased. Somehow she'd come all the way down the front steps and out to the quad cab without Addie noticing.

James broke the kiss, but he didn't let go of her. He wrapped an arm around her waist and drew her close to his side. "Don't know what it is about this woman. Can't seem to keep my hands off her."

"I noticed." Carm held out her arms. "Gotta go."

Addie slipped free of James's embrace to hug her sister goodbye. "I'm so sorry you had to stay so long, but I'm so glad you came. And Dev, too. Give him my love, and tell the kids that Auntie Addie will see them soon."

"I will." Carm stepped back. "You need us, you call. Don't you dare hesitate."

"I won't."

Carm looked toward the ranch house. "I have a feeling PawPaw's going to be okay now."

"Me, too."

"And I really like Lola. She's smart and funny and she won't take any crap off him."

Addie grinned at that. "I think you're right."

Carm turned to James. "Ready?"

He pulled open the front passenger door and Carmen got in. "I'll be back by six or so," he promised, those blue eyes warm as a summer sky. "You want me to bring takeout?"

She shook her head. "I bought groceries Tuesday when I got Lola settled in. We're having roast chicken, baked sweet potatoes and green salad, totally heart healthy for PawPaw's sake."

He hooked his hand around her neck again and pulled her close for another kiss. "You are an ideal granddaughter."

"Tell PawPaw that."

"I have. And you just might be the perfect wife."

"Call me amazing. Go right ahead."

"Amazing." He whispered it. The sound reached out and touched her in all her most hungry, sensitive places.

She kissed him. It started out as a light, brushing caress. But it just felt so good. With a sigh, she wrapped her arms around his neck and deepened the contact.

Inside the quad cab, Carm tapped on the passenger window. *Knock it off*, she mouthed. *Let's go.*

James kissed her once more, quick and sweet, for good measure, then went around and climbed up behind the wheel.

Addie stood waving, Moose at her side, until the pickup rounded the first curve on the way to the highway.

Then she turned to her dog. "Lots to do." Moose tipped his head to the side and whined in doggy understanding. "Come on. We'll clear some dresser and closet space for James first. Then we'll catch up with the horses until it's time to get dinner going. If we're lucky, we may even have a little time to get out to the shed and get going on the orders." She needed to get to work on the garden, too. The window had arrived for planting broccoli, cabbage, cauliflower, peppers and tomatoes. She would start them in her little greenhouse out by her work shed. But that wouldn't be happening today or tomorrow. Maybe next week, if she was lucky.

Moose gazed up at her with those big brown eyes of his, listening intently, as though he couldn't wait for the next pearl of wisdom to drop from her lips.

She asked, "So, what do you think, Moosey?"

He took his cue and gave her a bark of encouragement.

She scratched his wide forehead. "Well, all right. Let's get after it, then."

Panting happily, he followed her back into the house.

"I still haven't seen the bill for the floor repair and the bath railings," Addie complained that evening.

James didn't answer her. He didn't plan to give her that bill.

They were in her upstairs bedroom. He'd brought more clothes from the condo and he was putting them away.

"James. Stop pretending you didn't hear me."

Tucking a stack of T-shirts in next to his boxer briefs, he shut the drawer and returned to the suitcase spread open on the bed next to his adorable short-term wife.

She caught his arm as he reached for a stack of sweaters. "I want that bill."

Grabbing her hand, he straightened and yanked her up into his waiting embrace.

"Stop that." She struggled, but not very hard.

He held her lightly. "Don't worry about that bill. I already paid for it and Garrett gave me a great deal." He tried to kiss her.

But she pressed her hands against his chest, craned back away from him and glared. "It is so wrong for you to pay to fix the hole that my grandfather made while he had you tied to a chair."

"It's not wrong if I want to do it. And I do want to do it. I'm over all that with the chair and the shotgun."

"You shouldn't be. I'm certainly not."

"Addie." He said it softly, coaxing her.

Stubborn as always, she looked away. But then she looked back. He could tell she was trying not to smile. "Oh, all right. What?"

"Let it go." He put on his most appealing expression. He hoped. "Please."

She kept trying to pretend she wasn't looking at him—but then couldn't seem to resist shooting him quick glances. "Let what go? The bill or what PawPaw did to you?"

"Both—and while you're at it, stop pushing me away."

She relaxed her arms, slid her hands up and clasped his shoulders. "Fine. I'm not pushing you away."

"Better. Let me pay for the repairs."

"It still seems—"

"Shh. Don't say anything more—except for yes."

"The insurance will pay for the grab bars if I can just send them the itemized bill."

"Well, all right, then. I'll get a separate bill from Garrett for the railings, you send it in and then when they pay you, you give me that check."

"But the floor... That had to be expensive."

"Let it go, Addie. Let me help a little. I'm living here with you rent free."

"Because I asked you to."

"I like it here."

"That's right." She widened her big eyes in pretend horror. "You poor man. As soon as you leave here you'll be forced to go live in that big, beautiful new house of yours."

He didn't want to think about leaving her yet. After all, he was just moving in. "You didn't even let me help pay for the groceries."

"You'll figure out a way to do that," she grumbled. "I know how you are."

"Let it go. Accept a few good things when they come your way. Say thank you. And then move on."

Her mouth got softer. So did those big eyes. "Thank you."

"You're welcome."

"You are so good to me—and to PawPaw."

"Only because I like you." He dared to reach out and trace the sweet curve of her cheek. She let him do it, a very good sign. He whispered, "Both of you. A lot." He tugged on her earlobe. "Especially you…"

She sighed then. And this time, when he bent to claim her lips, she didn't back away.

Eventually, with great reluctance, he let her go to finish putting his clothes away. She helped him hang his shirts, slacks and jackets in the closet.

Once that was done, he took her hand and pulled her over to one of the dormers and then down with him onto the window seat. Outside, the sun had just set, leaving a last gleam of daylight along the rims of the mountains.

She asked, "Did you see Elise when you stopped by to get your clothes?"

"I did. She and Tracy have agreed to stay at the condo for a while. But already, they're talking about finding new apartments. That's Elise for you. Too damn independent."

"There's nothing wrong with independence," she informed him smartly.

He grinned. "How did I know you were going to say that?"

And then she grew thoughtful. "I've been trying to think of what I could do to help. They don't by any chance need horses boarded, yummy fresh vegetables come summer or a free scarecrow?"

He tugged on a silky strawberry curl. "I'll tell Elise you offered—or you could tell her yourself. She'll be at our party."

She was gazing out at the sunset—but at the words *our party*, she whipped her head around to pin him with a look. "What are you up to now and which party is that?"

He caught her hand again. "It's like this. My sister Clara came to my office today. She's reserved the upstairs room at McKellan's for a week from Saturday night." Walker's brother, Ryan, owned and ran the popular Irish-style bar.

"They're all a little annoyed with me for getting married out of the blue."

Shadows filled those golden eyes. "You know, they're right. We should have told them."

"There wasn't a lot of time to send out wedding announcements. And they'll get over their annoyance. Especially if they can welcome you to the family with an after-the-fact wedding reception."

"Oh, James. What are they going to say when we suddenly separate in May?"

He lifted her fingers and kissed them, one by one. "Let's ford that river when we get to it."

"I feel guilty, you know? Like we'd be celebrating under false pretenses."

"Don't."

"But, James, I—"

"Just come to the party with me and have a good time. That's all you have to do. Clara says it'll be low-key. Nothing fancy or anything. They want to get together with you, welcome you to the family, celebrate a little, that's all. They're not going to judge us later because it didn't work out."

"Is that what you'll tell them? That it didn't work out?"

Now *he* was feeling a little annoyed. "I don't really know yet what I'll tell them. Do I need to know right this minute?"

"Well, of course not. I just mean…"

"What, Addie? What exactly do you mean?"

She slanted him a sideways look. "Am I upsetting you?"

"No," he firmly lied.

A big sigh escaped her. "It's so nice of them to do this." She sounded sincere—and also as though she might actually be about to say yes.

He'd been dreading this conversation all afternoon, had just known it would be hell trying to convince her. But she seemed at least to be considering the idea. He breathed a cautious sigh of relief and pushed for an affirmative. "So that's a yes? You'll come?"

A frown crinkled the space between her smooth eyebrows. "You would have to tell them no presents. You'd have to make it very clear. I can't stand the thought of them giving us toasters and nice glassware and who knows what all, and then feeling like I should send it all back when we're not together anymore."

He really wished she'd quit talking about when it was over. After all, it had barely begun. But he knew he had to let that go for now and concentrate on the goal of getting her to say yes to the party. "No presents. Not a single one. I'll get Clara's promise on that." He mimed an X on his chest. "Cross my heart."

And that was when she leaned close and kissed him, sweet as you please. "All right. Yes, I would love it if your family gave us a party."

Chapter Nine

The dress was cinnamon-colored, fitted close on top, gently skimming her hips and widening out to a flirty hem that came to just above her knees. Addie had sexy black heels to go with it and she felt like a million bucks as she turned to check out the back in the cheval mirror that had once been her grandmother's.

James, dressed in good jeans and a black dress shirt, whistled at her from the bedside chair. "Beautiful. Just beautiful."

She smoothed a hand down her still-flat belly. "I'm glad I get to wear it at least once before my stomach's out to here." She turned to him. "Thank you." She'd been working like crazy, trying to catch up on her orders, take care of the horses and get the early vegetables started in the greenhouse. They'd argued when he insisted she take an afternoon off last week. But as usual, he kept after her until she agreed to go. She was glad that he'd talked her into it. They'd had a great time in Denver, where he bought her both the dress and the shoes and then taken her out for Italian food. "Seems like I'm always saying thank you to you."

He got up and came to her, causing her breath to catch and her tummy to fill with small winged creatures. "I like you smiling and grateful." He tipped up her chin and looked at her as if he was considering eating her right up—something she really wouldn't mind in the least. "Scratch that. I like you any way I can get you."

"You are so easy to please."

"I can see how you might think that, because everything you do pleases me." He brushed his lips across hers. The man smelled like heaven—minty soap and a hint of aftershave. Too soon, he stepped back. "If I keep kissing you, I'll only want to take that dress right off you again."

"And we'll never make it to our party."

"Then my family will *really* be annoyed with me."

"Can't have that." She grabbed her clutch from the low bureau.

Downstairs, they stopped in the master suite to say good-night to her grandfather.

"Get over here, Addie Anne," Levi demanded from his fancy recliner bed. She held back a snappy reply and went to him. "Give your old granddad a kiss." Obediently, she bent down and kissed his cheek. When she straightened, he gave her a nod of approval. "You do look mighty fine."

"Thank you, PawPaw." She said it sweetly, thinking how much she loved him—even if she was still angry with him for all the wrong things he'd done. Moose got up from his bed by the bureau and came over to give her a sniff. She scratched his head. He licked her hand and then wandered over to get attention from James.

"Lola should be here to see you," Levi grumbled. The nurse had the weekend off—her first days off since she'd started taking care of Levi.

"Lola has a right to days off now and then," Addie chided.

"I know. But I've gotten used to her and I don't like it when she's not here." As a matter of fact, he already seemed to consider the nurse a part of the family.

Daniel, the relief nurse, rose from the chair in the corner and suggested briskly, "You need to keep busy. Let's take another walk around the house." He meant that literally. Every couple of hours, her grandfather got up and made a circuit of the ground floor. Lola insisted he take those walks religiously. And Daniel did, too. Moose would trail after them, wagging his tail.

Levi grunted. "The next torture session begins." He waved a hand. "Go on, you two. Have fun. Stay out late. Addie, no drinking. You have my future great-grandson to consider, after all."

McKellan's, on Marmot Drive in the heart of Justice Creek, took up most of the block between West Central and Elk Street. It had lots of windows and blue awnings that shaded outdoor tables in the summer months.

The pub was always busy. This Saturday night, it was packed downstairs, not a single seat available at the long mahogany bar, every table in use. A crowd waited near the hostess stand, everyone eager to get a seat.

James waved at the hostess and they went on past, weaving their way through the crowd to the open stairway that led to the party room on the second floor.

Clara, James's sister, was waiting for them at the top. A pretty brunette in her early thirties, Clara grabbed her brother in a hug. "There you are. Congratulations, James."

He beamed. "I am one lucky man and that is no lie." He said it as though he meant it. Addie tamped down the guilt that they weren't what they seemed to be and focused on being grateful for all he'd given her, for every day and night they shared.

Clara turned to her. "What a beautiful bride. Welcome to the family, Addie." She held out her arms and Addie went into them. Clara said softly, for her ears alone, "Thank you for making my brother a happy man."

Addie pulled back and met Clara's warm dark eyes. "I'm sorry we didn't even give you a heads-up. My grandfather was so sick. We were afraid he wouldn't make it…"

"No apologies necessary," Clara insisted. Then she asked hopefully, "But he's doing well now?"

"Much better, yes. Thank you."

By then, they were surrounded by Bravos. Addie got lots of hugs and a very warm welcome from each of James's siblings and half siblings. And from his cousin Rory McKellan and her husband, Walker, as well.

Rory grabbed Addie's hand and pulled her over to the upstairs bar. Addie ordered a club soda with lime and thanked Rory for taking such good care of her dog and her horses.

Best of all, when she offered scarecrows and fresh vegetables as a sort of thank-you gift, Rory said she would love a scarecrow. Rory's garden at the Bar N was fenced, but that didn't keep the occasional hungry crow away from the corn. "Plus," she added with a musical laugh, "scarecrows are hot right now, aren't they?"

"Very," Addie agreed. "And that's why I need to make you one. All you have to do is describe to me the scarecrow of your dreams."

"How about a lady scarecrow?" Rory asked. "With a big straw hat and an old-school gingham dress?"

"You want it country, you mean?"

Rory nodded. "Oh, yes, I do."

"I can so do country. I'll drop it by as soon as it's finished. A week, maybe. Two at the most..."

In the corner, a DJ was hard at work over a pair of turntables. Dance music filled the brick-walled party room. Addie got only one sip from her club soda before James was grabbing her hand and pulling her out onto the small square of dance floor. They danced several fast ones in a row. When there was finally a slow one, he pulled her close and they swayed in place, other couples pressing close.

"Hungry?" he asked her when the slow song was through.

"Of course." The past week or so, her morning sickness seemed to have vanished. Now she was hungry all the time.

He led her to the buffet table set up along the wall across from the stairs. They each loaded a plate and found seats at a table with his sister Elise and Elise's best friend, Tracy Winham.

Both women asked after Addie's grandfather and teased James because he'd finally settled down when everyone in the family had begun to wonder if he ever would. The two women tried to keep it light and easy, but Addie saw they were both under stress in the aftermath of the fire that had taken pretty much everything they owned. There were lines of strain on Elise's face and a faraway look in Tracy's eyes.

James asked what they planned to do about their catering business.

Elise replied, "As soon as the insurance pays off, we'll be looking for a new space so we can reopen."

Tracy jumped up as if someone had pinched her. "I could use another drink." And she made a beeline for the bar.

Elise, shoulders drooping, watched Tracy go with a bewildered expression on her face. Then she turned to James. "I don't want you to worry. We'll be out of your hair by the first of May."

He reached out and clasped her shoulder. "What did I tell you? I don't need the condo. Stay as long as you want to."

Elise's eyes turned steely as she hitched up her chin. "You've been a lifesaver. And we'll find our own place by May first." She bent close and kissed his cheek, a quick kiss—and final. Then she got up and followed after Tracy.

James leaned close to Addie. "Elise has always been way too proud for her own good."

It seemed to Addie that there was more going on with Elise and her friend than too much pride and a burned-down building. She said, "It must be awful, losing everything that way."

Before James could answer, Clara and her husband, Dalton Ames, president of Ames Bank and Trust, claimed the chairs Tracy and Elise had just abandoned. The four of them sat together for a while, talking casually about Clara and Dalton's eleven-month-old daughter, Kiera, about Levi's improving health and how much he liked his nurse Lola. As it turned out, Clara had been the one to hire Lola after Great-aunt Agnes's hip surgery.

James said, "I think Levi's got a crush on Lola."

Clara laughed. "I think *I've* got a crush on Lola. She's amazing."

Addie agreed. "What's not to love? She's a dream with my grandfather. She knows when to push him and when to indulge him. Without her, I'm pretty sure I would have strangled him by now."

Dalton said wryly, "So I guess that makes her a life-saver in more ways than one."

By then, Addie had cleaned her plate. James asked her if she wanted to make another run on the buffet.

"Maybe later." She excused herself to find the ladies' room.

The small one upstairs was in use, so she went down to the main floor to try that one.

Triumph! She got in and found an empty stall just in time. Once that was handled, she washed her hands, ran a quick comb through her hair and hurried to rejoin the party upstairs.

She was almost to the stairs when a voice she knew too well said, "Addie Kenwright. Well, what do you know?"

Her stomach lurched. *Keep going. Don't even glance back.*

But then again, why run away from him? Why give him the satisfaction of thinking he mattered that much? He didn't. Not anymore, anyway. He was just proof, and that was all that he was. Proof that she didn't have what it took to make a real and lasting relationship with a man.

She stopped, spun on her pretty black high heel and gave Donnie Jacobs a big, fat smile. "Hello, Donnie."

He wore dress Wranglers and a shiny trophy buckle on his heavily tooled belt. "You are looking very hot, Addie Anne." He tipped his black Resistol at her and whistled slow and low.

She couldn't believe this. He was such a jerk. How could she ever have imagined herself in love with him? "Really, Donnie. I'm not the least interested, so don't even start." She forced a brittle smile. "You have a nice night now."

"Hold on a minute, babe." He grabbed her wrist. "Don't be mean now, sweet Addie. We both know you've missed me…" About then, he spotted her wedding ring. "Whoa, what's this?"

"Let her go. Do it now." *James.* He was coming down the stairs toward them, moving fast.

Addie whipped her hand free. "That's my husband, James," she said to Donnie with a lot more pleasure than she should have let herself feel. "He doesn't look too happy. You'd better get lost."

Donnie made a low sound—a kind of worried sound. He was lean and fit. But James was bigger. And the expression on James's face said he did not appreciate anyone manhandling his bride.

James came right to Addie. He wrapped his arm around her. "You okay?"

She looked up into his handsome face and wished with her whole heart that she could keep him all the way past May and into forever. But she couldn't keep him. She didn't have whatever it took to make forever work. And she *would* remember that this time. "I am fine. This is Donnie Jacobs. He was just leaving."

Donnie tipped his hat so fast, he almost dropped it. "Uh. Congratulations, man. I, er, hope you'll be very happy."

James just looked at him. He didn't say a word.

Donnie muttered, "Addie. You take care." And then he was turning, striding away.

James pulled her closer, pressed a kiss into her hair. "You want me to have a private talk with him?"

"I do not. But thank you for offering."

"It would be my pleasure."

She held his gaze. "No. I mean it."

"What did he do?"

She glanced up to the top of the stairs where one of his half sisters, the gorgeous one, Nell, leaned on the railing gazing down at them. "It's not the time or the place. Let's go back to the party."

He smoothed her hair, ran a finger down the side of her neck, a caress that reminded her acutely of how much she loved it every time he touched her. "You sure you're all right?"

She went on tiptoe and kissed him. "I am just fine, I promise you. Especially now that you're here."

James waited most of the night to ask her about Donnie Jacobs.

When they finally climbed into bed at quarter of three, he went for it. "So, what's the story with the douche bag in the black hat?"

Instead of answering, she rolled over good and close to him. He gathered her closer still. She wore tiny panties and a silky bit of nothing on top. He wanted to get them off her.

But he wanted her to talk to him more. "Addie?"

"Mmm?" She pressed a kiss against his shoulder.

"Remember what I told you about Vicki? About how I came out of that marriage sure I was never getting married again?"

"I remember. James, it's clear to me that your first wife was a piece of work. All those rules. You must have felt like you were living in a prison. And she didn't like your family. I mean, what's not to like about your family? That was just wrong of her, to try to keep you away from everyone you care about."

He ran his hand down her arm, loving the silky feel

of her skin, thinking he would never get enough of having his hands on her. "By the time it was over, I was pretty messed up."

"And I am not the least surprised."

"My point is it took me several years after the divorce to start figuring out that every woman isn't Vicki. Is it possible you have some idea that every guy is like that Donnie guy?"

She sighed and pushed away from him.

"Get back here," he whispered. She resisted, but only for a second. Then she let him draw her close once more. He rolled to his back. Restless, she tried to roll away from him. He kept his arm around her. Finally, she settled her head on his chest. The silence stretched out. He kissed the top of her head. "Talk to me."

She lifted up enough to meet his eyes. "Well, the truth is my track record is just not good. I'm like my mother. She never could find a man to love her and stay with her. I'm not... I don't know how to explain it. It's like I've got a part missing. The part that knows how to be in a relationship. Every time I finally give in and take a chance on a guy, he changes and can't wait to get away from me. Somehow I always end up with a broken heart."

"So you're saying that guy tonight broke your heart?"

"He's not the only one."

James waited for her to elaborate. When she didn't, he prompted, "Who else, then?"

There was more sighing. Over on the rug by the door, Moose's tags clinked together as he rolled over in his sleep. Addie rested her arm on James's chest and then braced her chin on it. "You'll think I'm such a loser."

He shook his head at her. "Those fools who hurt you, *they're* the losers."

She smiled then, a sad little smile. "My high school

boyfriend, Eddie Bolanger, and I were supposed to get married. He bought me a ring and we started planning the wedding. And then Eddie went out on me. I should have thrown his ring in his face. But no, I tried to understand, tried to talk with him about why he would do that to me, to *us*. He said he did it because I was too clingy and needy and he couldn't take it anymore. He dumped me."

"Bastard." He lifted his head off the pillow and pressed a kiss to the center of her forehead.

"I sure thought so. Then he married the girl he dumped me for."

"SOB. No doubt about it."

"I swore off men forever."

"Forever is a long, long time."

"Yeah, I know. And swearing off men didn't work anyway."

"Did you seriously think that it would?"

She made a cute little humphing sound and then went on. "For a while, it was fine. I hung with Brandon and my high school girlfriends in my free time and stayed away from temptation."

"But...?"

"Randy Pettier happened. I met him the night I turned twenty-one. Brandon and I went to Alicia's to celebrate." Alicia's was a roadhouse out on the state highway about five miles from town. "Randy tended bar at Alicia's. He gave me free birthday drinks and told me I was the girl of his dreams. I resisted falling for him for months. Brandon tried to warn me that I was doing it all over again, losing my heart to some guy who would only hurt me. But I kept going back to Alicia's and Randy kept coming on to me. One night I kissed him. And then I did more than kiss him. We lasted a little over a month, Randy and me. I was just gone on him, so sure that I'd found true love at last. Finally, one night at his place, I told him that I loved him. He didn't say it back. A week later, he decided he was tired of Colorado. He said he needed to 'move on.' He packed up his pickup and left. Never saw him again."

"Good riddance."

"True. But I didn't see that then. I cried myself to sleep night after night. Finally, I pulled it together and reaffirmed my vow never to fall in love again."

"And then you met that Donnie character?"

"Yeah. Donnie's a cowboy. He works the local ranches, wherever he can find a job. And he loves the rodeo."

"I noticed the prize buckle."

"He means for people to notice it. He competes across several events. Including bull riding. That's where I first saw him. Riding a bull at the Justice Creek Summer Daze Rodeo. The guy is at his best with seventeen hundred pounds of bucking beef between his legs."

James laughed. "I take it you were impressed."

"Yes, I was. And I saw him in the beer garden later and he asked me to dance. For once, I showed a little backbone and said no. But then, suddenly, Donnie was everywhere. He got work on the Fitzgerald place. It borders Red Hill. And then PawPaw hired him to mend fences. Just seemed like I couldn't turn around without finding Donnie standing right in front of me. Over a period of about a year, I weakened. He asked me out a bunch of times before I ever said yes. But then I did say yes. Yes to dinner and a movie. Yes to spending every Friday night with him.

"I kissed him and fooled around with him. But somehow I kept myself from ending up in bed with him—or I did, until I finally decided that he was different and I needed to stop being so skittish and take a chance on him. One night he cooked me dinner out at this little cabin he was renting about ten miles from here. After dinner, we sat on the step and looked at the stars. He took my hand and gazed in my eyes and said he was in love with me. That did it. I confessed I loved him, too. We spent the night together…" Her voice trailed off. She laid her head down on his chest again.

James stroked her hair, rubbed a hand down her back. The room was way too quiet.

Finally, she drew in a slow, shaky breath. "In the morning, he cooked me breakfast. Then I drove back home with the radio on full blast, singing along to one corny country love song after another. I was so happy, James. I thought it had finally happened, that I'd found true love at last."

He rubbed her shoulder, ran his hand down the silky skin of her arm until he reached her hand and could weave his fingers with hers. "But…?"

"After that night, he stopped calling me and he never once answered the phone when I called him. I left him message after message. He never returned a one. I never ran into him out riding anymore. I tried to find him at the cabin. It was empty. If he was working for any of my neighbors, I never knew about it. By then it was summer again. So I went to the Summer Daze Rodeo and followed him to the beer garden between events. I walked right up to him and asked him what had happened, what went wrong. He said he'd never meant for things to get so serious and that we needed to take a break from each other for a while, start seeing other people."

James squeezed her hand. "I really should have decked that jerk."

"No, you shouldn't have. You were wonderful and calm just like you always are. He took one look at you and knew he couldn't take you. So he turned tail and ran. Totally worked for me."

"So that was it, then, with him, when you found him in the beer garden and he said he wanted to see other people?"

"Yep. Tonight's the first time I've set eyes on him since then. And if I never see his smug face again, it'll be way too soon."

James completely understood now why she'd kept him at a distance for all those months before Levi stepped in with his shotgun. She had no faith in her own judgment when it came to men. "So, then, after the bull rider...?"

"I swore off men for the third and final time—well, except for you."

He almost started to feel hopeful.

Until she continued. "But you are a special circumstance. I mean, if we *have* to be married until PawPaw recovers, at least we deserve a little fun in the bargain."

James said nothing. He was trying to figure out why he felt hurt. They *were* having fun. It was nothing like with Vicki. He was loving every minute of being Addie's short-term husband. Days, he looked forward to coming home to her. And the nights? Well, he and Vicki had had a lot of problems, but sex wasn't one of them. In fact, he'd never found a woman to match his ex in bed.

Until Addie. And Addie was so much more than just amazing in bed. She was also sweet and funny and tender. And she could be tough if you messed with her. He liked that about her, too. Her toughness and her sharp tongue kept things edgy and interesting. He was an easygoing guy at heart and he needed the kind of woman who kept him on his toes.

And maybe that was his problem here.

She'd figured out what she wanted in her life, had a

baby on the way and no inclination to try again long-term with any guy. When Levi had threatened to give up and die if she didn't marry James, she'd done what she had to do. And then turned right around and made the best of the situation. The way she saw it, they were simply enjoying themselves for as long as the marriage needed to last.

But for him it was different. Somewhere in the past few weeks, he'd gone way beyond just having a great time playing house with her. At first, he'd only tried not to think about it ending.

And now?

Now he loved it so much with her, he thought about the end all the time. Dreaded it. Hated it.

The bald truth was that he never wanted it to end. He wanted to keep on being Addie's husband for the rest of their lives.

Chapter Ten

The days were zipping by much too fast, Addie thought. Her marriage would be over in no time.

And James wasn't making it easy to think about letting him go. He was too good to her. Sometimes she wondered how she'd ever gotten along without him.

Which was downright ridiculous. She'd made it twenty-six years, after all, without depending on any man—well, except for her grandfather, when she was small. She could take care of herself and her coming baby just fine on her own.

Still, it was lovely having James around. He just had a natural tendency to pick up any slack, to help out whenever or wherever he might be needed.

Most mornings, he got up before dawn with her and helped her with the horses. He said that, growing up, he'd spent a lot of time out at the McKellans' ranch with Walker and his brother, Ryan, so he'd learned early to ride and to take care of horses. He claimed it made him feel useful to help her feed and groom them.

And the afternoons he got home early from town, he would show up at the shed where she made her scarecrows. He would haul in the bales of straw she needed for stuffing, or go digging through the boxes of old clothes she kept handy, trying to find the shirt she wanted or the perfect hat.

Sometimes she would look at him and feel that warm, expanding sensation inside her chest. She knew that feeling, the one that in the past had led inevitably to her saying *I love you*.

Well, she wouldn't say it this time. Those three little words were a great big jinx for her and her poor heart. She just needed *not* to say them and things would be fine.

Levi was doing really well. He grumbled and griped, but Lola just smiled and made him do his exercises and eat the heart-healthy foods Addie cooked.

Little by little, Lola had reduced his pain meds. He complained that his chest bone was killing him. That every breath he took, every time he coughed, every breathing exercise she put him through, every workout session—all of it was agony. She replied that agony was part of getting well and the pain meds only delayed the process, not to mention the dangers of addiction and constipation.

Addie and James both tried not to laugh when Lola got to the part about constipation. Levi would always get huffy and mutter that he damn well didn't want to talk about his bowels.

And Lola would come right back with "And we don't *have* to talk about your bowels, because we have your pain medication under control."

"What's this *we*, woman? *I've* got nothin' under control. *You're* the one who runs everything around here."

"Which is as it should be because I am your nurse, hired to see that you take care of yourself."

"I don't want to argue with you. It makes my chest hurt."

"Then stop. And come with me. We'll take a walk around the house…"

And he would mutter and swear, but he would get up from his fancy bed and take that walk with her, Moose falling in behind them, wagging his tail as they went.

Two weeks after the engagement party at McKellan's, Addie and James took Rory's new scarecrow out to the Bar N. Addie had gone all out with a blue denim jumper over a floral-patterned blouse. The flour-sack face had blue eyes, puckered red lips and pink cheeks with freckles. From yellow yarn, Addie had fashioned a wig with a long braid down the back. She'd added a wide straw hat with a big silk peony stuck in the band. As a final touch, she'd looped several long strands of fake pearls around the broomstick neck.

Rory loved it. They put it up in her garden and she said it was about the cutest scarecrow she'd ever seen.

The day was warm and sunny. Addie had packed lunch for four and suggested a picnic. Rory and Walker said they were in. So they tacked up four of the Bar N horses and set out toward the mountains, following the trails on the edge of the national forest. Eventually, they chose a spot in a sunny meadow just starting to green up now that the snow had melted. They spread their blanket and shared lunch.

Rory really was a great person, Addie thought, not the least pretentious. You'd never peg her as a princess if you didn't already know that she was the youngest daughter of the sovereign princess of Montedoro.

The Bravo-Calabrettis were not strictly royal, Rory explained. They were princes, and that meant they claimed a throne but not a crown.

To be royal, somehow, there had to be a crown involved. Addie didn't really get all that and said so.

Rory laughed. "Most people don't. Go ahead. Call us royal if you must." She went on to describe a little of what it had been like to grow up in the world-famous Prince's Palace perched high on a hill overlooking the Mediterranean Sea.

That following Monday, the last one in April, Addie got a package from Carmen in the mail. Dev had printed up the pictures of Addie and James's wedding. Carm had mounted them in an old-fashioned wedding album. Addie turned back the fancy padded white cover and there she was with James, both of them in their wedding best, holding hands by Levi's hospital bed in front of the pastor. Just the sight of that first picture tore her heart in two. Tears clogged her throat and a choked sob escaped her.

No. She was not going to break down crying like some hopeless romantic fool.

She slammed that cover shut and carried it straight upstairs, where she stuck it in the hall linen closet under a stack of towels. If she looked at even one more picture of her and James's wedding day, she knew she'd end up bawling like a baby.

Time was passing way too quickly. In less than a week, it would be May. In two weeks or so, Lola would be leaving. Levi's health improved daily. He took long walks outside now, him and Lola and Moose. It wouldn't be long before he had no more need for a nurse.

And her marriage to James? They'd agreed it would last two months. As of now, they were more than halfway there. Before they knew it, she would have to let him go.

The next day, when she went grocery shopping in town, she bought a pretty Hallmark thank-you card. She scribbled a little note inside to Dev and Carm, saying how great PawPaw was doing and how much she loved the wedding album—no, she did not mention that she'd glanced at only the first picture and then stuck the thing away in the linen closet to keep herself from collapsing in a crying jag. Some things her sister and her brother-in-law just didn't need to know.

Three days later, she got the certificate of marriage in the mail. She carried it right upstairs, stuck it in the wedding album and then hid the album back in the stack of towels in the dark. Yes, it was foolish to get so emotional over some pictures and a marriage license. And she felt a little guilty that she didn't mention either to James. He would probably need the license to file for their divorce. And he might get a kick out of seeing the pictures.

Too bad. She just couldn't bear to have to deal with those pictures. And the sight of the marriage license made her heart hurt.

Carm called a little later that day, before James got home from the office. Addie was able to thank her sister again for the album without worrying that James might hear what she said and ask questions later.

"You sound weepy," Carm said. She'd always had an annoying way of knowing when Addie got the blues.

"Uh-uh," Addie replied. "I'm not weepy in the least."

"Is it James?"

"Didn't I just say there's nothing wrong?"

"Yeah, and you're lying. Is it about James?"

"James is the best there is." He really was. "I'm crazy about him and he treats me like a queen." All true, if not the whole story.

Carm bought it. "Oh, honey. I'm so glad your marriage

is going so well. See? I told you that there really are good guys out there, that you just hadn't found the one for you yet. And now you know what I was talking about. You're a good match, you and James."

More guilt on her shoulders. She'd never exactly told Carm that she and James had agreed to stay together for a set period of time.

And she really didn't feel up to discussing it now. Yes, putting it off was cowardly of her. Too bad. She'd do it later, after James had moved out. "James and I are getting along great." That part was true, at least.

"PawPaw making you miserable?"

"Nope. He's getting better every day. His chest still hurts and he complains about it constantly, but that's to be expected. Lola takes good care of him and he adores her. When she's not here, he has Daniel to look after him. I hardly have to do a thing."

"Hormones, then, right? Don't you have an ultrasound coming up?"

Addie ignored the first question and went with the second. "I do. A week from tomorrow, as a matter of fact."

"Feeling okay physically?"

"Carm, will you give it up? I mean it. I'm fine."

They talked a little longer, about how good business was at Dev's sporting goods store, about how Addie's niece and nephew, Tammy and Ian, were both doing well at school. After that, Addie said goodbye and ran to Levi's room to tell him that Carm was on the phone. He picked up his bedroom extension and Addie returned to the kitchen, where she got to work on dinner.

Faintly, from the master suite, she heard her grandfather's chortling laugh. The sound cheered her. He really was getting well and her life was back on track.

It wouldn't be easy, giving up James. But for now, she

would just keep moving forward and try not to dwell on what the future would bring.

James got home half an hour later. He came straight to the kitchen, where she was putting zucchini, tomatoes and onions on to steam.

"There you are." He slid one arm around her waist and smoothed her hair out of his way with his free hand. Heaven, the heat and strength of him at her back, the feel of that hard arm wrapped around her. Then he bent close and kissed the side of her neck. He whispered, "You are the most delicious woman." And then he nibbled a line of kisses downward toward the crook of her shoulder, setting off lovely flares of sensation as he went.

She put all her dark thoughts of losing him away and let out a low laugh. "Delicious, am I?"

"Yes, you are."

A silly giggle escaped her. "Don't ruin your dinner now."

"How about if I just make *you* my dinner?" He turned her around. She put her hands against his broad chest, looked up into those dark-rimmed blue eyes and couldn't help wishing that things could be different, that their marriage could be what Carm and PawPaw believed it to be: real and lasting, true and strong.

It could be, chided a voice her head. *Possibly. If you'll just step up and ask for it. If you'll only put your heart on the line one more time.*

Oh, she wanted to do that so bad that she could taste the longing on her tongue, a sweet taste, but bitter, too.

Because she *had* stepped up before. And encountered only heartbreak every time.

But James...

James is different, nothing like the others.

He bent close and kissed her.

Yes. Perfect. Nobody kissed the way James kissed.

But hadn't she thought the same of Eddie's kisses, back in high school? And Randy's and Donnie's, too?

Wasn't she, really, something of a love junkie? She got addicted so easily, and then she crashed and burned.

He kissed her again. She could have stood there in that kitchen and kissed him for hours. Or better yet, grabbed his hand and led him upstairs, where they could lock themselves in her bedroom and do more than just kissing.

But PawPaw needed his low-fat, nutritious dinner. And the vegetables weren't going to steam themselves.

She kissed him once more and said, "Have a beer and let me get this dinner on."

He took a cold one from the fridge and set the table for the four of them. "I talked to Elise today," he said as he set the plates around.

"How's she doing?"

"Great, she says. I don't know if I believe her. She told me that she and Tracy had a long heart-to-heart." He went to the flatware drawer and counted out the knives and forks and spoons, then carried the silverware to the table and started setting it out at each place. "Tracy said she's never been happy in the catering business. She wants to go into the master's program in molecular biology at the University of Washington."

"Whoa." Addie put on her oven mitts and checked the pork roast. Done. Careful not to spill the drippings, she eased the roasting pan onto the top of the stove, shut the oven door and turned it off. "Molecular biology? Tracy? Where'd that come from?"

"Tracy's always been something of a science whiz. But she and Elise are pretty much joined at the hip, and have been since they were in diapers. My mother and Tracy's mother were best friends. Tracy was eleven when her mom and dad died. She moved in with us. She and Elise were constantly together, a unit, closer than twins. Elise leads, Tracy follows."

"Not anymore, apparently."

"Elise says she wants Tracy to be happy and that she's fine reopening Bravo Catering on her own."

Fine. It was a word Addie had been using way too much lately. *I'm fine* and *it's all fine*, when really it wasn't. *She* wasn't. In reality, she was spinning in circles emotionally, longing to tell James what was in her heart, knowing from hard experience that telling a guy how she felt about him was a bad, bad idea.

He said, "Elise and Tracy have both found apartments. It's official—they're moving out of the condo on the first of May. I don't really get that, why they had to scramble to get new places. I told them they could have the condo for as long as they wanted."

"I know." She set the mitts on the counter. "You did what you could. But you know how it goes. People do what they feel they have to do."

He'd finished setting the table. He picked up his beer, took a sip, set it down at his place and went to her at the stove. "So, how was your day?"

"Uneventful." *Except that our marriage certificate came and I hid it in the closet with the wedding album you will never see. And then I lied to Carm and told her that everything was just fine.*

Some hint of her uncertainty and heartache must have shown in her face. He frowned down at her. "You okay?"

She smiled up at him as though she hadn't a care in the world. "I am fine."

His frown disappeared. "You certainly are." He bent close for another quick kiss, after which she sent him to tell Levi and Lola that dinner would be ready in ten.

* * *

Addie was sitting on the front step, her arm around Moose, when James got home from the office the next day. He knew instantly from the haunted look in her amber eyes that something had happened.

He got out and went to her. "What is it? What's wrong?"

"Sit with me?"

He dropped to the step next to her. Moose got up from her other side, went around and plopped down next to him.

He scratched the dog behind the ears and asked again, "What's the matter, Addie Anne?"

She leaned her head on his shoulder. "I got a call from Brandon's lawyer in Denver a couple of hours ago. He wants me to come to his office on Monday at ten. He wouldn't tell me what it's about, just said he'd explain everything then." A small groan escaped her. "Why is it that bill collectors and lawyers and doctors with bad news always get in touch on Friday afternoon to let you know about scary stuff you can do nothing about over the weekend?"

He smoothed a hand down her hair. "Just consider this…"

"What?"

"Could be that it's good news."

"James, he called on *Friday* afternoon. Didn't I just explain to you that no good calls come in on Friday afternoon?"

He hooked his arm around her hip and snugged her up nice and close. She'd been working with her scarecrows. She smelled sweetly of the fabric softener she used on the flour sacks she stuffed to make the scarecrow heads. "I'll drive you."

She sucked in a sharp breath and looked up at him, big eyes soft and grateful. "Would you?"

"Try to talk me out of it." He brushed a kiss between her eyebrows.

"I don't know why I'm so nervous. I mean, how bad can it be? I did kind of worry that maybe there was some problem with the insurance."

He remembered that Brandon Hall had set the Kenwrights up with a trust to pay hefty health insurance bills for the next several decades. He shook his head. "If there was an insurance issue, you'd hear either from the insurance company denying a claim or from the hospital letting you know that they haven't been paid."

"I got the first statement. It all looks good—the bills are enormous, but all of PawPaw's care is being covered, including Lola, who is totally worth the big bucks she's getting."

"So, then, don't worry. Whatever it is, we're going to find out on Monday. Maybe Brandon left you something more than the insurance."

"No. He left it all to a foundation he established to help kids like he used to be, kids with acute medical conditions growing up in foster care."

"Hey." He wrapped his arm around her neck and used his thumb to tip up her chin. "Do not—" he pressed a kiss on those plump lips "—worry."

Her smile was like the sun slipping out from behind a dark cloud. "I won't. Now that you're coming with me, I'll feel like I have a lawyer of my own."

"Because you do." And he kissed her again, but slowly that time, savoring the taste of her, loving the way her breath hitched and she wrapped her arms around his neck and slid her fingers up into his hair.

When he lifted his head, she looked up at him with eyes full of stars. "Thanks."

"For what?"

"For working so hard to convince me that everything will be all right."

"It will be." One way or another, he would make sure of that. She got up and held down her hand. He took it and stood. "What's for dinner?"

"Leftovers. Let's go in. I'll cut up the salad and you can set the table."

James made sure Addie arrived at the lawyer's office at five minutes of ten on Monday morning.

A secretary ushered them into a small conference room, where a blue folder waited with Addie's name on it. James pulled back the chair for her and she sat, her hands in her lap, looking down at the folder as though she feared it might bite.

James took the chair beside her and leaned close. He was just about to have a look in that folder to see what this was all about when Brandon's attorney appeared in the doorway.

"Good morning."

"David," Addie said with a nod. She introduced James. He reached across and shook hands with the other lawyer, whose last name was Pearson. Pearson sat down, too. He had a blue folder of his own.

Addie shifted nervously. James leaned into her and rested his arm on the back of her chair. She sent him a wobbly smile and then faced the other lawyer. "Okay, David. Will you please tell me now what this is about?"

Pearson opened his folder. James reached over and opened the one in front of Addie. It was Brandon Hall's will.

Brandon's lawyer explained, "I'm sorry to have made this such a mystery, but Brandon wanted it that way."

Addie sent James another glance, confusion in her eyes. Then she asked Pearson, "But why?"

"A week before his death, Brandon sent for me."

"Because…?"

"He said he wanted a change to his will and he didn't want you to know about it until three full months had passed after his death."

"Three months. That would've been Saturday," Addie said softly, wonderingly. "He died three months ago this past Saturday."

"That's right."

She made a frustrated sound. "I just don't get it."

James leaned even closer and gave her arm a reassuring squeeze. "Let him explain."

She gulped and sighed. "Sorry, David. Go on."

Pearson said, "Brandon told me that he wanted you provided for, but the most you were willing to accept from him was the health insurance trust he arranged for you and your family and any children you might have. He said that every time he tried to tell you he was leaving you a large monetary bequest as well, you became upset and said absolutely not."

"The insurance fund alone is so generous," she insisted. "More than enough. I let him talk me into that. I refused to accept more until we knew for certain that there was going to be a baby. And then he died suddenly. We had thought he had at least a few months left…"

David Pearson asked gently, "So there is a child?"

"I'm pregnant, yes."

He looked from Addie to James and back to Addie again. "Brandon Hall's child?"

Addie let out a laugh that sounded a lot like a sob. "It's a long story. But yes, I'm having Brandon's baby. And James and I got married a little over a month ago."

Pearson said, "It's unfortunate that Brandon didn't live to know he would be a father. But the child's existence has no effect on the will in front of you. The bequest is to *you*, Addie. Brandon Hall was adamant that you should be provided for, child or no. The document before you takes care of that. He told me he knew that you would be upset enough at his death. He didn't want to have you confronted right away with the fact that he'd left you a large sum of money, which you had insisted you didn't want. His wish was to give you time after his death to grieve and accept his passing before springing this bequest on you."

Addie bent her head. "Oh, this is just so…Brandon." Tears clogged her voice, frustration, too. And love. She really had loved Brandon Hall. James sucked in a slow breath and reminded himself that he would not be jealous of a dead man who had only wanted to make sure she was taken care of after he was gone.

Pearson said, "If you'll turn to page five, you'll see that the bequest is a generous one and that the inheritance taxes are already paid." When Addie just sat there staring at the open folder, James turned the pages for her.

At the sight of all those zeroes, Addie cried, "Oh, James…" She groped for his hand. He gave it and she held on tight. "Is this really happening?"

"Yes, it is," said Brandon's lawyer. David Pearson was smiling.

Addie said, "I think I maybe need to pinch myself." She turned those big golden eyes on James. "Sometimes I…" She gulped. "Oh, it's silly. Never mind."

"It's all right," he coaxed. "Go ahead. You can say it."

"Well, especially since PawPaw's heart attack, I've been so worried about all that could go wrong."

"I know…" He gave her hand a squeeze.

"We've always managed all right, PawPaw and me. We really have. But the hard truth is that we're getting by month to month. There's not a whole lot left over for emergencies. Even knowing that we had the cost of Paw-Paw's medical care covered, I still worried constantly the whole time he was in the hospital. I kept telling myself not to freak out about all the orders I wasn't filling, about owners moving their horses elsewhere because I wasn't there to take care of them."

"I know," he said again, though there'd been no need for her to worry. Saintly Brandon Hall wasn't the only one who would see to it that she was taken care of no matter what. Whatever happened in the end between him and Addie, *he* would have made certain that she and Levi and the baby had everything they needed to get by.

And wait a minute...

What exactly was he feeling here?

Pissed off.

Yeah. That was it. He felt pissed off—angry at a dead man who'd done nothing but see to the future well-being of someone he cared about.

That was pretty damn small of him.

And it got worse. He was not only pissed off at Brandon Hall's generosity; he'd actually been counting on Addie's sketchy finances, at least a little, hadn't he? He'd been counting on all he could offer her that she didn't have, counting on her needing to turn to him for help whenever things got tight.

He hadn't admitted that to himself until right now because he'd never needed to admit it. Until right now, it had only been a simple fact: she didn't have a lot of money and he had plenty and of course he would help her in any way he could.

But now the truth came way too clear.

She wasn't going to need James to take care of her. Brandon Hall had left her enough that she could take care of herself and her family in style. As of today, Addie could say goodbye to worrying about how to make ends meet.

Thanks to Brandon Hall and his millions, she would never want for anything again.

Chapter Eleven

Addie left the lawyer's office with her copy of Brandon's will and a check so big she felt kind of faint every time she looked at it. She sat in the passenger seat of James's quad cab clutching the blue folder with the check paper-clipped inside it and wondered if this was all just a dream.

"Let's stop for lunch and celebrate," James offered before he started up the truck.

"I couldn't eat a bite. Not until this check is safely in my bank."

"Straight to the bank, then?"

"Um, yes, if that's all right? It's Ames Bank and Trust." Of which Dalton Ames, Clara's husband, just happened to be president.

"Dalton's bank." James echoed her thoughts.

"Yes. And I would like to go to my own branch, the

one in Justice Creek. It's been our bank since PawPaw was young."

"That's a lot of money…"

"Oh, no kidding." She thought of all those zeros again and tried not to hyperventilate. "So what? You have a suggestion?"

He nodded. "Why don't you let me call Dalton and he can tell us if it's better to go to the main branch here in Denver for this—kind of give the bank a heads-up?"

"That's a good idea." She gave him a grateful smile. "Yes, please. Call Dalton."

He used the car's speakerphone to make the call. As it turned out, Dalton Ames was right there in Denver that day. He said he would meet them at the main branch.

James drove them over there and Clara's husband took them into his fancy office and personally put her giant check into savings for her. It didn't take long. Dalton promised she'd have access to her money within a few days. She left with a handful of pamphlets offering her various investment opportunities.

When they were back in the quad cab, she said, "Now. Let me take *you* to lunch. Pick the place. Money is no object."

"Big spender, huh?" he teased.

"Oh, you bet. Steak? How about steak?"

"I know just the place."

He took her to the legendary Buckhorn Exchange, where the red walls were covered in mounted big game, the tables had old-timey checked cloths and you could get not only prime aged beef, but also buffalo, elk and alligator tail. The Buckhorn Exchange had fabulous steaks and double-chocolate rocky road brownies for dessert and for the first time in her life, she didn't even blink when she got a look at the check, just handed over her credit card and added a generous tip.

On the way home, she started thinking about all those investment brochures from the bank. "James?"

"Hmm?"

"You told me once that you do asset protection."

"That's right. I'm in business and family law."

"But I mean…that money I just put in the bank is one wonkin' asset."

"It certainly is."

She glanced over at him. He was watching the road, his profile looking sterner, more serious than usual. "What's the matter?"

He turned and gave her a quick, warm smile before focusing on his driving again. "Not a thing."

Did she believe him? It seemed something had been bothering him. She decided not to pressure him and returned to the subject at hand. "Ahem. Will you help me to figure out the smart things to do with all the money? Will you be my lawyer for real? Advise me, you know, so I don't mess up and lose it all?"

He laughed then, a low, sexy sound that made her want to reach out and touch him—run her fingers up into his thick hair and wrap a possessive hand around the nape of his neck. "Addie, you're much too frugal to go throwing your money away."

"But you hear about it all the time. How people who don't have much get a windfall and they go kind of crazy and it's all gone in the blink of an eye."

He looked her way again, his blue gaze steady. Calm. Oh, she did love that about him. That calm at the center of him, like a cool blue pond in some secret mountain glen. It always reassured her, made her feel that no matter how rough things could get, with James around, it would all work out in the end.

Don't leave me, she thought and tried not to let her yearning show on her face. *Don't ever go.*

But of course, he would go. And she would *let* him go. Gracefully. Without making any big scenes.

"We'll talk about it," he said and put his attention back on the road. "Discuss possible investments and your comfort level with risk."

"Risk?" She wrinkled up her nose at the word. "James, I don't like risk."

"Well, then, it will be pretty simple. Savings accounts, savings bonds, CDs, the kinds of investments that are very secure but pay small dividends."

"I don't need big dividends and I like that word, *secure*."

"Okay, then. You can take your time about it. No need to rush into anything."

"There is one thing I keep thinking about."

"Say it."

"Well, I'm at three months now, with the baby. Riding horses from the second trimester on can be dangerous. So I'm thinking maybe it's time I hired someone to help with the animals and to handle some of the chores around Red Hill."

"Addie Anne, you could get yourself an army of hired hands."

She grinned at him. "No, really. I think for now just one will do."

He drove her back to the ranch, dropped her off and then went on into town to check in at his office. Moose came running out to greet her. She dropped to a crouch and hugged him good and tight and whispered, "Oh, Moosey. We're rich. Do you believe it?" The dog panted and wagged his tail as though the happy news pleased him no end. "Come on. Let's go tell PawPaw."

But when she went inside and knocked on Levi's door, he called out in his grouchiest voice, "Is the house on fire?"

"No, PawPaw. I just want to—"

"I don't care what you want, Addie Anne. *I* want to be left alone."

"Well, fine. Be like that." She'd tell the old meanie the big news later. As she turned from the door, it opened and Lola came out, closing it quietly behind her.

Addie asked, "What's put a bug in his butt, anyway?"

Lola's composed smile did not reach her eyes. "I told him this morning that Friday will be my last day taking care of him. He's doing so well, Addie. Even his chest has finally stopped hurting. He can walk a good distance at a steady clip." Addie knew Lola was right. Over the weekend, he'd helped her out in the garden. He'd been managing light chores for over a week now. "He's eating well and off the pain meds," said Lola. "He really doesn't need a nurse anymore."

Levi's bad attitude suddenly made perfect sense. "He's upset that you're leaving."

"He's become…somewhat attached, that's all."

Addie wanted to hug the older woman—and why shouldn't she? She reached out. Lola didn't turn away. She stepped forward and for a moment they held on tight. Addie felt the tears itching at the back of her throat. It was stacking up to be a pretty emotional day. "You know, I think I've become attached, too. I don't want you to go, either."

Lola gave a shrug, the movement both sad and resigned. "I'll miss you both. *And* that handsome husband of yours." Moose, at Addie's feet, let out a whine. Lola patted his head. "And you, too, Moosey. I'll miss you, too." She met Addie's eyes again. "But that's the nature of my job. Just when I feel as though I'm part of the family, it's time to move on."

Levi refused to come out of his room for the rest of the day. When James got home, Addie told him that Lola was leaving at the end of the week and that Levi was angry about it.

They put the dinner on the table and then she had James go in and tell Levi and Lola that the food was ready. Addie expected her grandfather to go right on sulking, to refuse to come to dinner like a naughty five-year-old.

But he came to the table.

Too bad that when he got there, he made them all wish he'd just stayed in his room. He was awful. He ignored his meal. Folding his arms across his chest, he glared at Lola.

Lola was amazing about it. She smiled sweetly back at him and appeared to enjoy her trout, green beans and salad enormously. Addie guessed it was all an act, but still. She admired the nurse all the more for not giving her grandfather the satisfaction of knowing he was getting to her.

Finally, when all that surly glaring didn't work, Levi took his rudeness to a whole new level. "Give me that sweet smile all you want to, Lo, I know you're scared." *Lo?* PawPaw called Lola *Lo?* That was kind of…intimate. Addie zipped a glance at James. He looked as bewildered as she felt. Levi went on. "You aren't really the heartless bitch you keep pretending to be."

Addie gasped. "PawPaw. What is the *matter* with you?"

Before he could answer, Lola let out a cry, jumped to

her feet and threw down her napkin. "That does it, Lee. That simply takes the cake."

Addie whipped her head toward James again and mouthed, *Lee?* Wide-eyed, James shook his head, his surprise a match for hers.

PawPaw stared up at Lola, a hot smirk on his thin lips. "What? Don't tell me. For once you're actually going to admit how you feel?"

Lola sucked in a hard breath. And then, her face flaming red, all her usual cool composure fled, she cried, "You petulant, spoiled old fool. I could…could… Oh, you just make me want to throw back my head and shout this house down!" And with that, she turned and fled through the family room.

"Lo! Lo, you get back here!" Levi jumped to his feet, fast as he ever had before his heart attack. He took right off after her.

Addie asked James, "What is going on?"

"Hell if I know."

They got up simultaneously and trailed after Levi and Lola.

From down the short hall to the master suite, Addie heard Lola cry, "No! No, Levi, this is wrong. It's so unprofessional…"

And her grandfather came right back with "You're done, remember? You're not my nurse anymore."

"But I—"

"Shh, Lo. It's all right. I know I've been an ass. But I couldn't make you listen."

"Lee, I can't—"

"Yeah. Yeah, you can. Please don't fight it anymore. I love you, sweetheart. And I promise you, we're gonna make it work, gonna find the happiness we both deserve. Lo, it's gonna be all right…"

Another soft cry followed. And then there was silence.

Addie and James just gaped at each other.

About then, either Levi or Lola must have realized they'd left the bedroom door open. Somebody gave it a kick.

Addie startled as it slammed. "Well," she said softly. "PawPaw and Lola. Should I have guessed?"

"Probably." James took her hand and led her back to the breakfast nook table. They sat down and picked up their forks again.

Addie ate a green bean. "I never did get around to telling him about the money." She sighed. "Maybe tomorrow."

James sipped from his beer. "He's looking pretty spry, your grandfather. Bounced right up out of that chair and chased right after her."

"Lola did say he doesn't need a nurse anymore."

James sent her one of those smiles that warmed her inside and out. "He still needs Lola, though."

"Yep. I think he really does. And from what just happened, I'm guessing that maybe she needs him, too."

The next morning at breakfast Levi announced, "Lo is no longer my nurse. I fired her." He reached for Lola's hand. She gave it and he kissed the back of it. "She's not my nurse, and she's not going anywhere."

Lola colored like a youngster. "We want to spend time together."

"Lots of time," said Levi. "So she'll be staying here at the ranch house with me."

Lola added, "And if I'm not here, he'll be coming to stay at my house. But we'll also take time alone, too, so we each get some space."

"Not too much damn space," Levi muttered.

And she chuckled. "No, darling. Not much space at

all." She said to Addie, "When you get older, you find you don't want to waste a minute that you might spend with the person who means the most to you."

Without stopping to think twice, Addie looked to James. His blue gaze was waiting. They shared a glance that felt so tender. So right.

The old folks were in love. And so was she. And she really, really wanted to speak of her love with James.

Yes, she had promised herself not to go there ever again. But some promises, well, didn't they just beg to be broken?

If her grandfather could find love again after so many lonely years, didn't that just prove that love was something you should never give up on?

Addie swallowed down the tears that always seemed to be so near the surface lately. She said, "I'm so happy for you two," and she meant it with all her heart.

James nodded in agreement and Levi and Lola beamed with happiness.

That evening at dinner, Addie finally told her grandfather of the visit to Brandon's lawyer and the enormous sum of money Brandon had settled on her.

Levi didn't seem the least surprised. "I knew he was filthy rich, that boy—and don't get prickly, Addie Anne. I mean 'filthy rich' in the nicest way possible."

"Oh, PawPaw," she chided.

The wrinkles in Levi's brow deepened. "But I thought you said you refused to take any of his money."

"He left it to me anyway."

Her grandfather said very gently, "Well. God rest his soul."

Addie was sorely tempted at that moment to bring up the baby again, to try to get her grandfather to admit, at last, that she hadn't lied, that Brandon *was* the baby's father and her grandfather had kidnapped an innocent man—and then forced her and James to marry by threatening to let himself die.

But why ruin a really good moment with accusations and anger? James claimed he was over it.

And PawPaw was almost eighty. He'd survived a massive heart attack and found true love again at last.

Let him have his illusion that James was her baby's father. In this case, she doubted that the truth would set anyone free.

A little later as she and James were clearing the table, a rolling boom of thunder sounded outside.

"Storm coming," she said.

James set down the two plates he'd carried to the counter and moved to stand behind her. He wrapped his arms around her.

He was brushing a lovely line of kisses down the side of her throat when thunder rolled again and she warned, "Don't tempt me."

"I live to tempt you..." He kissed the words against her skin.

She turned her head back over her shoulder and they shared a swift, hot little kiss. "I have to hurry, get my sleeping bag and get out to the stables."

He frowned at her, confused. "Because...?"

"You know Dodger?"

"That big bay gelding, you mean?"

"That's the one. He goes wild when there's a thunderstorm. Weather report said it might storm, so I put him in a stall for the night just to be safe. If I leave him in the pasture, he's been known to jump the fence and run off. But I need to get out there and make sure he doesn't hurt himself kicking at the stall."

"I thought you were going to hire someone to help you with the horses."

"I have. I called around and found a dependable man who's worked for us before, but he can't start till next Monday, so I'm on my own tonight."

Out the breakfast nook window, lightning flashed, followed by a rolling boom of thunder. She kissed him one more time and then made for the mudroom. "Just leave all that," she said over her shoulder of the half-cleared table. "I'll deal with it in the morning."

He followed and stood in the doorway to the kitchen as she grabbed her hooded canvas jacket off the peg by the back door. "You'll be sleeping out there tonight?"

"Probably." She grabbed some wrinkled apples from the bin under the mudroom sink and stuffed them in her jacket pockets.

He said, "I'll finish clearing off and be with you in ten minutes."

The idea delighted her, but it was only fair to warn him, "You'll be a lot more comfortable upstairs in bed."

"Uh-uh. Where you are. That's where I want to be."

Addie stopped by the storage shed and got two sleeping bags. It was starting to rain as she ran for the stables. Slipping in through the outside door, she tossed the sleeping bags in the corner.

Dodger gave a snort, followed by a nervous whinny of greeting. She went to his stall and spoke to him soothingly. He snorted twice more but seemed to settle a bit.

"Good boy, good boy." She fed him two of the apples as the rain came down harder, drumming on the rafters overhead.

Dodger let her pet him and whisper to him.

When it seemed safe to leave him for a minute, she went

to unlatch the doors that led into the pasture, pushing them open just wide enough that she could look out. Through the veil of the rain, she could see the other horses huddled in the run-in shed, an open-sided structure that provided shelter during bad weather. They should be all right.

As she pulled the doors shut again, lightning blazed and thunder roared. Dodger neighed and kicked the stall door, hard. She went back to try to soothe him, waiting till he danced around to face the stall door again, then getting hold of the halter she'd left on him just for this purpose.

He kept rearing back, trying to jerk free. But she held on and blew in his nostrils and petted his fine, long forehead with its pretty white blaze. "Shh, it's okay. You're okay now, boy…"

She'd just gotten him settled when the thunder roared again. With a squeal, he pulled free and started kicking the stable wall behind him, tossing his head so she couldn't catch the harness.

And then there was James beside her, his hair wet from the rain, wearing his heavy quilted jacket. He had the extra height and longer arms to catch the harness again.

Addie caught the other side. Together, they whispered soothing words until Dodger finally settled once more.

The rain drummed harder on the roof. Addie heard Moose whine. Still holding her side of Dodger's harness, she glanced over to see the dog sitting by the sleeping bags, tongue lolling, expression hopeful.

James stroked Dodger's muzzle and followed her glance. "He came out of Levi's room looking for you, so I brought him along."

More thunder.

They both focused on the horse again, holding on,

petting him, whispering that he was safe, that everything was okay.

The rain kept on coming down. But after fifteen minutes had passed with no more claps of thunder, Dodger seemed calm enough that she gave him another apple for being such a good boy. Then she and James went to spread some clean straw on the floor and lay out their sleeping bags.

James had brought a couple of blankets and two pillows. They used the sleeping bags as a bed and the blankets to cover them.

"Very cozy," he said, when they lay together on their mattress of straw, with Moose stretched out contentedly beside them.

She had her head on James's chest and her hand on his heart, with his strong arm around her, her very favorite place to be. "You showed up at just the right moment."

He pressed his lips to her hair. "We make a good team."

Her heart did something impossible inside her chest. "Yeah," she agreed in barely a whisper. She tipped her head back to smile at him. "We really do." *And I love you so much and I'm terrified to tell you that—scared to death that when I do, everything will go wrong.*

He bent a little closer. "Addie, I—"

She pressed a finger to his lips, her stomach going hollow with fear—of what he might ask of her, of the things he might say that she might answer in kind. Last night, seeing her grandfather and Lola all dewy-eyed, in love as two teenagers and admitting it openly, anything had seemed possible. Last night, for a little while, she'd actually believed that she could say her love out loud to James and it would all work out.

But right now, as he looked at her with tender intentions, right now, with the moment upon her…

Uh-uh. No.

These things never worked out for her. She couldn't bear to go there again and have it all go bad. She didn't even want to think about it.

Not tonight, anyway.

"Don't talk," she whispered. "Just kiss me."

"Addie." He said it tenderly—and reproachfully, too. "We can't go on forever without—"

She cut him off. "Kiss me, James."

He shook his head, but then he did give in. Their lips met. He gathered her close.

Outside, the rain poured down. Moose gave a big yawn. In his stall, Dodger shifted with a low sound very much like a sigh.

James pushed at her jacket. She let him take it away and then helped him get rid of his. It didn't take long to shed all their clothes. James pulled the blankets over them.

He laid his big, warm hand on her belly. "You're a little bit rounder here, I think…"

It was true. She had a tiny baby bump now, though it was nowhere near big enough to show under her clothes. Laughing, she elbowed him in the side. "James Bravo, are you calling me fat?"

"I'm calling you beautiful." And then he kissed her again.

It was so sweet and right, just the two of them, the rain drumming overhead, making love, saying things with their bodies that she could never quite bring herself to put into words.

Addie told herself that was okay. It wasn't that she would never tell him. It was only that she wasn't ready yet, to say it, to find out if this time really was as different as it seemed to be. She had two weeks yet until their two-month marriage ended. Surely by then she would find a way to say that she loved him and wished with all her heart that he might stay.

Thursday, Levi spent the night at Lola's house in town.

Friday morning, it was just Addie and James at the ranch house. They got up before dawn, as always, and tended to the horses. Back inside, he cooked them breakfast and she set the table.

When they sat down, he asked her what she had planned for the day. She told him about the orders she needed to work on, the weeds she needed to pull in the garden and that she had her second ultrasound at Justice Creek General at one.

He gazed across at her so steadily and she had that scary, wonderful feeling that he could see right down inside her heart. And then he asked in a worried tone, "Is something wrong, then? With you? With the baby?"

"No. Honestly. This is an optional ultrasound for me. More and more doctors are advising that women have them at eleven to thirteen weeks. There's really no indication that ultrasounds hurt the baby or the mother. It's totally noninvasive. It uses sound waves and not radiation. And at thirteen weeks, they can check for issues like Down syndrome and other genetic disorders." He'd gone from worried-looking to slightly alarmed, so she added, "James. It's okay, I promise you. I have no reason to believe the baby has any of those things. I just think it's a good idea, to check everything that can be checked. Plus, I might be able to find out if it's a boy or a girl—that's not real likely this early, but it's possible."

"It's at one, you said?"

"That's right."

"I want to be with you. I'll meet you there."

James wasn't sure, exactly, why he wanted to be with Addie for the ultrasound.

He just felt that he should be there, that he wanted to see those shadowy sonogram images, see for himself the tiny person inside Addie that had somehow changed everything. Because of the baby, Levi had kidnapped him. Everything, really, had started from there. If not for that awful day when Levi had his heart attack, James doubted he'd ever have had a chance with Addie.

Sometimes he still doubted that he really had a chance. She was scared to go all the way with her feelings. She'd been hurt more than once revealing her heart and she wasn't eager to try that again.

James got that. He did. He kept trying to figure out how to talk about forever with her.

But he hadn't managed it yet. Something always held him back. He wasn't sure exactly what. Maybe the way she still guarded her heart. When he held her and made love to her, she gave herself completely. But somehow she made it so that the moment was never right to talk about where they might go from here. He didn't want to ruin what they had by pushing too fast.

For the ultrasound, Addie lay on a padded exam table in a darkened room. The technician, whose name was Kate, slid the gel-smeared probe in slow, exploratory circles over her bare belly.

James stood beside Addie, across from Kate and her keyboard and the sonogram screen. On the screen, the images flickered and changed. They heard the baby's heartbeat, a hundred and sixty beats per minute.

And then, for a second, a glimmer of a shape that

might have been a human form. Slowly, as Kate worked the probe, the image came a little clearer. James could make out separate body parts beyond the overlarge head. He saw tiny arms, hands, fingers—even toes. Kate said the baby was only three inches long, that fingerprints were starting to form, that reflexes had begun to develop, that the baby could hiccup and yawn and swallow, that the kidneys were just beginning to function.

"Did you want to know the sex?" she asked.

Addie said, "Yes."

Kate slid the probe around in a slowly narrowing circle. "See that? He's not shy."

A boy, then? James thought maybe he saw something that just might have been a penis, but then it was gone. "You just said 'he.' So it's a boy?"

Kate the technician answered with a firm "Yes."

"A boy," Addie repeated with a happy little sigh.

James stared at the tiny figure floating inside Addie, watched the little guy flex his transparent fingers, wiggle his miniature feet. Brandon Hall's baby.

But somehow, strangely, *his* baby, too.

Was he out of line, to think that?

He didn't see how.

With Brandon gone, the little guy could use a dad.

I can do this, he found himself thinking. *I can be this baby's dad.*

He not only *could*, but he *wanted* to. Like a warm and welcoming light going on inside that shadowed room, as he watched the thirteen-week-old baby on the flickering ultrasound screen, everything changed again, the same as it had changed the day Levi tied him to a chair.

That barely formed baby had James seeing with perfect clarity that he had no more need to be jealous of Brandon Hall and his money. Brandon had loved Addie.

Brandon had done all he could to protect her, to take care of her after he was gone. And Addie had loved Brandon, too. But not *that* way, not the way she could love James if she would only let herself. Addie needed *him*, James, no matter how afraid she was to claim him.

And this tiny baby? This baby needed him, too.

And all that was just fine with James. Because he needed both of them.

Now if he could only make Addie believe that he did.

James waited for the right moment to tell her that he loved being married to her—he loved *her*, damn it. That he wanted to be a dad to the baby she'd made with Brandon Hall. He wanted the life *they* had made together. He wanted it all with her until death did them part, which he expected to be a long, long time from now.

Unfortunately, that moment never came. Somehow she always found a way to silence him before he even started talking. She did it so cleverly, with a sweet kiss, or a deft change of subject—or the sudden absolute necessity to be off and doing something in another room.

The new hand, Rudy Jeffries, came to work on Monday. He brought two of his own horses and a single-wide house trailer to live in until Addie could get the foreman's cottage across from the main house fixed up for him. Tuesday, Addie had a plumber and an electrician out to add hookups for the trailer on a pretty grassy space not far from the barn.

That night, she told James how good it felt, to whip out her checkbook and pay for what was needed without batting an eye. Wednesday, she called Nell to get Bravo Construction out to tell her how much it would cost to make the needed repairs to the foreman's cottage and some upgrades to the house, as well.

The following Monday, when she got the formal estimate from Nell, she freaked out a little. The total for everything she wanted done was well over fifty thousand.

That night in bed after they made slow love, James held her and soothed her and reminded her that she was rich now. He teased, "Fifty K is chump change."

She got all prickly. "I do not like throwing money away, James."

"You'll like it less when the foreman's cottage caves in from neglect. Plus, it's about time you got a new kitchen and an overhaul of that basement room."

She snuggled in closer. "You're right. I know you are…"

It seemed a perfect moment to bring up their future. "Addie Anne, I—"

She lifted herself right up and put a finger to his lips. "Sorry, but I really have to pee. Be right back." And she jumped from the bed, scooped her short robe off the bedside chair and disappeared into the bathroom.

No way was he waiting even one more day to talk about the future. According to the original agreement they'd made, their supposed two-month marriage ended on Thursday. He had a feeling if he just let things go without insisting they talk about it, they could wander on into the future together without ever saying the words that meant so much.

But he didn't want it like that between them. He wanted her to know how he felt, what he wanted with her, how precious she was to him. He wanted to tell her that he would like to be a father to the baby, to say all the words that mattered so much when two people decided to make one life together. He also wanted to hear those words coming back to him out of her sweet, plump mouth.

He turned on the lamp, propped his pillow against the headboard and sat up to wait for her.

Took her a good ten minutes to return. She hovered out of the circle of the lamp's light, her big eyes wary, arms wrapped around herself as though for comfort. Even through the shadows he could see her quick mind working. She didn't want to ask him why he'd turned the light on, because he just might tell her that he wanted to talk. Then she'd have to invent some new excuse to shut him up.

He broke the silence. "Come back to bed, Addie Anne."

She started chewing that sweet lower lip. "Oh, James…"

"We have to talk about it." He patted the empty space beside him.

"Please." The distress in her voice was way too evident and she hadn't come any closer. "We have a few more days. Can't we just enjoy them?"

He didn't like the sound of that at all. But this time, he was getting the damn words out no matter what she did to stop him. "We can have forever and you know it."

"James—"

"No. You're not going to stop me. Not this time. I love you and I want to stay with you. I want the baby, too. I want it all with you, Addie. I don't want it to end and there is absolutely no reason that it has to end. We're married and we can stay that way. I want that. And I want you to tell me that you want it, too." Yeah, all right. As declarations of love went, it lacked finesse. But still. He'd meant every word and he hoped, at least, that his sincerity came through.

She shifted from one foot to the other, let her arms drop to her sides and then rewrapped them around herself. But she didn't come to him. She stayed in the shadows. "I'm just… You're such a good man. I… You're everything, James. But I'm not going to say it. Saying it never works for me. Saying it only makes everything go bad."

"Will you listen to yourself? You know that's not true."

"I just… I *can't*, James. I'm not going to say it. It's not going to happen."

He had a really bad feeling. A feeling that she meant it, that she never would say it, never would let herself get past what Donnie Jacobs, Eddie Bolanger and Randy Pettier had done to her heart. "You're smarter than this, Addie. And I'm not like any of those jerks who messed you over."

"I know you're not. You're good and true. But it's like a jinx for me, you know? I say it, and everything goes wrong."

"That's not going to happen with me, with *us*."

"I'm sorry." She did take a step closer then, into the pool of light cast by the lamp. He held his breath as she raised both hands—and then let them drop to her sides. "No, I just can't. I really can't."

He kind of wanted to break something. But he tried another tack instead. "So, then, what's going to happen? How do you see this playing out? Are you thinking that on Thursday, I'm just going to pack my stuff and move out?"

She shut her eyes. "I don't know. The truth is I don't want to think about it. I *never* want to think about it."

He held out his hand. "Come here."

She did look at him then. And she let out a hard, shaky sigh. "I feel like such a complete loser. I mean, I'm a woman. Women are supposed to be good at all this, at dealing with emotions, expressing their feelings…"

"Come here."

At last, she came. She even put her slim, work-roughened hand in his and let him pull her onto the bed beside him.

"Take off the robe."

She pulled the tie. It fell open.

He pushed it off one shoulder and then let go of her hand in order to ease it all the way off. "Lift up." She lifted up from the mattress enough that he could get the robe out from under her. He tossed it onto the chair a few feet away. She looked so beautiful and so sad, sitting there naked, unable to let herself say what he wanted most to hear. He held up the covers and she slid beneath them. He settled them over her and pulled her into his arms.

"I'm sorry," she whispered against his heart.

He stroked a hand down her hair, cupped the velvety curve of her shoulder. "Be warned. I'm saying it again. I love you. That's *my* choice, to love you. I chased you for all those months before Levi took the situation in hand and made it so I could catch you—at least for a while. In all those months before your grandfather came after me with his shotgun, I never had a prayer with you, did I?"

"I just couldn't." Her voice was so small, he almost didn't hear it. "I just never know what I'm doing when it comes to—" she had to swallow before she could say it "—love. I always mess it up."

"You haven't messed a damn thing up. But you haven't had a chance to choose, either, have you—not when it comes to you and me?"

She tipped her head back. Those amber eyes met his. "What are you getting at?"

"That *I* chose *you* the first time you rode that gray mare past my new house."

"Oh, that's just crazy."

"Maybe. But it's also the truth. I saw that ginger hair

escaping out from under your hat, shining in the sun, saw the perfect, curvy shape of you astride that pretty horse. And then you stopped and you smiled at me. We started talking. By the time you rode away that day, my heart went with you."

Her eyes shone brighter, the shine of tears. One escaped and trailed down her round cheek. "Oh, just look at me. Crying." She sniffed. "I'm not only a loser, I'm a wuss, a complete wuss."

"No, you're not." He brushed at the wetness with his thumb. "And I don't want to make you cry, Addie Anne. But I do want you to have your chance to make *your* choice, a choice you make not because I won't stop chasing you and not because your grandfather threatens to die unless you marry me—die like Brandon did. And your mom, too. That was so cruel of Levi to do that to you."

She pressed her lips together hard, wrapped her fingers around his upper arm and held on too tight. "You are planning something, James. I know you are and already I don't like it, whatever it is." He kissed the tip of her upturned nose—and she accused, "You *are* leaving me, aren't you?"

"I'm moving to my new house, that's all. I'm moving there loving you with all of my heart. And I will be there, waiting, hoping that you decide it's safe to believe—in me and in you and in the life we can have together."

"It's what I said," she whispered again, that plump lower lip trembling. "Dress it up however you want, make it sound like you're doing me a favor. You. Are. Leaving."

"What matters is I love you. And yes, on Thursday, I'm moving to my new house, where I will be waiting, praying every damn day that passes that you will give yourself a chance to trust me, that you will come and get me. That you will make *your* choice to take me as your husband for the rest of our lives."

Chapter Twelve

Addie longed to beg him to stay.

But she didn't. She knew he was nothing like Eddie or Randy or Donnie, knew that he really did care for her, knew that what she had with him was deeper, truer and more real than anything she'd had with any man before.

Still, she shed that one tear right when he told her he would go—and after that, well, something went numb in her.

She didn't want him to go, but of course he *would* go. She'd known that all along, now, hadn't she?

At least this time she hadn't made a fool of herself. He'd even said he loved her and somehow she'd managed not to say it back. That had always been her brilliant plan if any man ever said those three little words to her again: not to say them back.

So she'd followed through with the plan.

And it didn't feel so brilliant, after all. Truth was, it

felt even worse than declaring her love and ending up with a stomped-on heart. It seemed to her by then that something really had gotten broken inside her. She'd lost that special, sacred part of a person that knew how to love and be loved in return.

Would she ever be mended?

She just didn't know.

The morning James left, he hugged her and kissed her and whispered, "Take care of yourself, Addie Anne." She stared up at him, wordless, until he dropped his cherishing arms and stepped back.

"Bye, James," she managed at last.

PawPaw came out on the porch right then. Addie waited for him to throw a fit. After all, the shotgun marriage he'd threatened to die for was ending so easily, with James walking away and Addie planning simply to stand there and watch as he drove off and left her.

Levi offered his hand to James. They shook and Levi pulled James close to pound his other hand on James's broad back. "Don't be a stranger," said Levi gruffly, as though James had just dropped in for a visit and now he was heading off back to his own life.

Well, and maybe that was exactly what was happening here.

Tell him you love him. Beg him to stay, pleaded the lovesick fool within.

But she wasn't going to do that.

And on second thought, she wasn't standing there on the porch to see James drive away, either. She slipped past her grandfather and went into the house, shutting the door quietly behind her.

Inside, she waited for Levi to come stomping back in and read her the riot act for letting James go.

Didn't happen. PawPaw came in. He asked gently, "You all right?"

"No, I am not and I don't want to talk about it."

"Fair enough." He headed for the kitchen. Addie trailed along behind him, not sure what to do with herself. He went straight to Lola, who stood at the sink loading the dishwasher after their breakfast. He wrapped his wiry old arms around her and kissed her neck.

That did it.

Addie whirled around and left the room. The last thing she needed right at that moment was to see a pair of happy lovers kissing on each other.

She went out to the stables, but there wasn't much to do there. Rudy was conscientious and good at his job. So after hanging on the pasture fence and petting the horses that came to say hi, she went on to her work shed and spent the morning stuffing flour-sack heads, painting faces on them and assembling the outfits for her next several orders.

That day passed. And the next one. The weekend dragged by. Three times, she started to take off her wedding and engagement ring set. She should have given them to James before he left Thursday morning. But she hadn't even let herself think of such a thing then.

And now, well, she couldn't bear to do it. So she just went on wearing them, telling herself that eventually she would have to take them off and return them to him.

It hurt so much—the vast emptiness of her own bed at night, the space at the table that didn't have him in it, the words she needed to say to him that he wasn't there to hear.

And his touch. And his kiss. And the scent of his aftershave.

How long would it take her to get over James Bravo?

She really, really needed to stop asking herself that.

Monday, Nell Bravo came with a crew to start fixing up the foreman's cottage. Nell was well-known in her family for speaking her mind. Addie worried that James's half sister might demand to know what had gone wrong with her and James. But Nell only gave her a big hug and asked her a few questions about the teardown and went to work with her crew.

Another week dragged by. That following Monday, the final one in May, Addie drove into town for groceries. She stopped at the bank and arranged with the branch manager to put some of her money from Brandon into CDs, which were safe and low risk. Because she didn't do well with risk. Not when it came to money.

Or her heart, apparently.

Once that was done, she considered the amount left in her savings account. She'd hardly made a dent in it. So she transferred another fifty thousand into her checking account. She went home and sent money to the Wounded Warrior Project, the ASPCA, UNICEF, the Salvation Army and the family shelter in town.

She felt a little better after giving some of her windfall to people who needed it and she decided she would make a habit of giving regularly.

But did writing those checks help her get over James? Not one bit.

Two more weeks went by. She talked to her sister twice on the phone. Carmen didn't like it that James had moved out, but when Addie asked her to leave the subject alone, Carm didn't argue, either.

Addie met Rory in town for lunch. Rory asked how she was doing. Addie said she was managing all right. Rory offered to listen if Addie had needed to talk. Addie thanked her and said she would think about it. They left it at that.

The days ran together. Addie worked on her orders, approved of the progress Nell and her crew were making on the cottage and started thinking about more stuff that could stand doing around Red Hill. She hired another hand to work three days a week. He would mend fences, help Rudy when needed and clear brush to keep the danger down in fire season.

Addie's stomach grew rounder. She wished James were there to put his big hand on it and smile at her in that special, tender way that only he did. She ached to drive by his house and see how he was doing.

But she stopped herself. What would she say to him? Nothing would do for him but *I love you* and she was too much of a coward to ever say those words again.

The second week of June, she had her eighteen-week ultrasound and missed James desperately all through it. He would have loved to see the baby now. The little boy had grown to five and a half inches. Addie watched him kick, roll and flex his arms, activities she'd already felt him doing in the past couple of weeks.

She couldn't button her jeans anymore. So the next week, on Friday, she went into town and bought actual maternity clothes. She was putting them away in her closet and bureau when she heard footsteps along the upper hall.

PawPaw appeared in the doorway to her room. "Addie Anne, we need to have us a talk."

Whatever he had to say, she didn't want to hear it.

She still hadn't forgiven him for kidnapping James and causing his own heart attack—and then forcing her and James to the altar by refusing to get well.

"Please," he said, his eyes, the faded blue of worn denim, so sad.

She went over, plopped to the edge of the bed and gestured at the bedside chair. "Have a seat."

He came into the room and eased himself down into the chair. "How you feelin'?"

Except for my hopeless broken heart? "Fine, Paw-Paw. Truly."

"Good. You look good—except for that sad face you're wearing all the time."

She asked him wearily, "What is it you wanted to talk about?"

He folded his gnarled hands and twiddled his ancient thumbs. Finally, he came out with it. "I know that my new great-grandson is Brandon Hall's baby. I knew since that day in the hospital when you brought me all those damn papers from that sperm bank and your doctor."

Addie sat very still for a second or two. And then she accused, way too softly, "You knew and yet you *still* wouldn't get better until James and I got married?"

The white head dipped once in confirmation. "I knew he loved you and I knew you would never give him a chance to make you happy. Not unless somebody took the matter in hand. So I did what I had to do. But I know that what I did was wrong and I'm thinking you're never going to forgive me. I could live with that, with you hating your old PawPaw for the rest of my days. Except that now you've sent James away. Now you haven't got love and you're mad at me, too."

"Serves you right," she muttered. "And at least out of the wrong you did, you found Lola. I'm glad for that."

"Lo is my miracle and I thank the good Lord daily for the gift of her love. But what about *your* miracle, Addie?" When she only swallowed hard and looked away, he said, "James and I had a long talk, before he left."

"I'd wondered about that," she said to the far wall. "I figured something had gone down between you two when you just let him go with a handshake and a pat on the back."

Levi grunted. "He made me admit how wrong I was to threaten to die on you unless you married him. He made me see that you blame yourself for your mother's death—though that was not in any way your fault—and then you also lost Brandon. And the men you loved before, well, they weren't worthy of you. So you had been hurt again and again. And I piled more hurt on you. It was a very bad thing I did, to blackmail you with the threat of dying on you. I only made everything worse for you, harder for you, when I did that, only battered your heart around all over again."

She looked at him then. How could she help it? The hard knot of anger within her at him? It was melting away like an icicle in the morning sun. "You know I forgive you. You're everything to me, PawPaw."

"I'm old, is what I am. And I won't be around for all that long."

That numbness inside her—where had it gone? Her heart ached. Tears welled. She gulped them down hard. "Please don't say that."

His smile was the sweetest she'd ever seen. "Don't be afraid. I'm not planning to go *that* soon."

"Good."

"Addie, I want you to have your true love before I go. I would do a whole lot of wrong all over again, God forgive me, if you would just go to James and tell him what's in your heart for him. If you would just bring him home to Red Hill, where he belongs."

"Oh, PawPaw. What if he's changed his mind by now?"

Levi gazed at her patiently. "I promise you he hasn't—and that's not to make light of your fear. Lovers do leave and the people who mean the most someday will die. But in the meantime, when you find the one for you, you need to grab hold, Addie."

She saw the truth suddenly. "I fulfilled my own fear, didn't I? I *made* him leave."

"But the good news is he loves you."

"He…he did say he would be waiting."

"So, then, you only need to master the fear in you. Master the fear, go after him. And once you get him, hold on tight."

The next morning was Saturday. James woke up again in his dream house.

In the month since he'd left Addie, he'd furnished the place just the way he liked it, with comfortable and attractive high-quality furniture in the neutral colors he preferred. He liked the way the kitchen faced the mountains and the back deck was wide and welcoming, with an outdoor kitchen to rival the one inside.

It was all exactly as he'd dreamed it would be.

And he hated it.

Because Addie wasn't in it with him. Because it wasn't the house at Red Hill.

Was he losing hope that she would come for him?

Maybe. A little.

Was he considering saying to hell with giving her the time to make her choice and just going after her? So what if he was? If she was going to make the *wrong* choice, well, where was the good in that?

Those were the questions that chased themselves around in his brain constantly now. The only thing that kept him from going after her was the promise he'd made her: to let her do her own choosing in her own time.

First thing, he made coffee with his brand-new pod machine and he carried a full cup out to the front porch as he did every morning, to sit on the step and stare off toward Red Hill and tell himself that today was the day Addie Anne would finally appear on his doorstep to tell him she loved him and wanted him to come home.

She wasn't out there.

But his heart did a forward roll in his chest anyway.

Because a scarecrow in a business suit sat on the front porch swing, his arm around a lady scarecrow in denim overalls, with a roundness at her waistline that could only mean the lady scarecrow was about to have a little pile of straw. The husband scarecrow had a white picture album in his lap.

James set his coffee on the little table by the swing and picked up the album. Inside the front cover was his and Addie's marriage certificate, complete with the seal of the Arapahoe County Clerk. Legal and binding. He smiled to himself at the thought and turned the next page and then the next, taking his time, thumbing through the pictures of him and Addie on their wedding day.

They both looked so happy. As though the wedding really was the real thing and what they both wanted.

Because they *had* been happy. And it had been exactly what *he* wanted, at least.

And the scarecrows in the porch swing had him thinking she was finally admitting that she wanted it, too.

Carefully, he set the album back down in the lap of the scarecrow. He picked up his coffee and took a sip of his favorite morning blend. His knees felt a little wobbly—with hope and anticipation, with the thrill of knowing she had to be somewhere nearby. He went to the front steps and sat down. The coffee sloshed in his cup; his damn hand was shaking. Carefully, he set the cup beside him, up against the porch post, where he knew it wouldn't spill.

Only then did he dare to say her name. "Addie."

For endless seconds there was nothing. And then he heard her footsteps, light and quick as ever, coming around the corner from the side deck.

There was plenty of room on the step beside him. She dropped into the empty space, filling it with everything that mattered in the world.

His vision fogged over with unmanly tears. He didn't dare to look at her. "Addie," he whispered, as if it were the only word he knew.

She took his hand. Nothing had ever meant so much as that—her hand in his, guiding his palm to rest on her belly.

"Rounder," he said, his voice a sandpaper rasp.

"James, I…" She seemed unable to go on. But then she did. "I got here an hour ago, set out the scarecrows and then couldn't quite manage to knock on your door. I've been sitting in a chair on the side deck, trying to get up the nerve to face you. I'm such a wimp…"

"No, you're not."

"Yeah, I am."

He couldn't stand anymore not to see her face. Slowly, he turned his head. "Where's your horse?"

"I drove the pickup, left it around that bend in your driveway." She pointed toward a clump of ponderosa pines not far from the house. "It seemed so important, that you see the scarecrows first. And the wedding album. Carm sent it about two months ago. I stuck it under some towels in the upstairs hall closet, hid it from you."

"And from yourself?"

A little hum of agreement escaped her. She stared off toward the pines and confessed, "I hid the marriage license, too. That was silly, huh? Like hiding what we really are to each other would make it so I never had to tell you what I'm so afraid to say."

"You can do it," he said gently. "I know you can."

She turned her head to gaze at him again. Her golden eyes shone and her soft mouth trembled. And then, at last, she gave him the words he'd waited so long to hear. "I...don't like my life without you. I miss you so much, it hurts. I...well, I *have* made my choice and my choice is *you*, James. I want you to come back to me, please. I want you as my husband and a second father to my baby. I want us to have *more* babies—I mean, if you want that, too..."

"You bet I do."

"I...I love you, James." A small cry escaped her. "There. I said it." She squeezed her eyes shut, quivered out another breath—and opened her eyes again. "You're still here."

He felt the welcoming smile break across his face. "Damn it, Addie. I was getting worried." He couldn't wait a second longer. He reached for her.

"James." She melted against him with another, happier cry.

"Addie, Addie…" He buried his face in the crook of her neck and breathed in the yearned-for scent of her. "I love you. Only you. Always."

She held on so tight. "I love you, too. I love you, love you, love you, I do."

He took that sweet mouth of hers then, in a kiss he would never forget for as long as he lived. A kiss of reunion, a kiss that promised she would take him with her, home to Red Hill.

A kiss that said she was ready at last to take a chance on forever.

With him.

After the kiss, he got up. She rose beside him. He took her hand and led her into the house. He showed her the rooms and the back deck and the outside kitchen.

And the master bedroom, too. They spent an hour in there, celebrating their reunion. It was by far the happiest he'd ever been in that king-size bed.

Afterward, they dressed slowly, stealing kisses as they buttoned up and pulled on their boots, laughing together like a couple of kids.

"This house is beautiful," she said once they had all their clothes back on and sat on the bed side by side.

"I think we can get a good price for it," he replied with satisfaction.

"But…do you want to live here? I would be happy to live here. It's such a fine house and it's right next to Red Hill."

He lifted her hand and kissed the back of it. "It was my dream house."

"I know. And I mean it. Let's live here. As long as we're together, I'm happy wherever we are."

"No."

"Are you sure?"

"Yes. Dreams change, Addie Anne. I don't want to live here anymore. We belong at Red Hill. I want us to raise our family there." He pulled her close for another sweet, endless kiss. When he lifted his head, he said, "Give me five minutes. I'll pack up a few things and we'll go home."

* * * * *

Watch for MS. BRAVO AND THE BOSS,
the next installment in Christine Rimmer's
THE BRAVOS OF JUSTICE CREEK *miniseries,*
coming in October 2016,
only from Harlequin Special Edition.

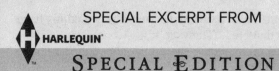

SPECIAL EXCERPT FROM

HARLEQUIN

SPECIAL EDITION

*When pregnant single mom Sasha-Marie Gibault
returns home after her divorce, she reconnects with her
childhood crush, Graham Robinson. But the rancher's
interest in this little family is jeopardized when they
learn he may really be a famous Fortune.*

Read on for a sneak preview of
WED BY FORTUNE,
the final installment in the 20th anniversary miniseries,
**THE FORTUNES OF TEXAS:
ALL FORTUNE'S CHILDREN.**

"I'm so proud of the woman you've become." He trailed
his fingers along her upper arm, setting off a rush of
tingles that nearly unraveled her at the seams.

What was going on? Why had he touched her like
that? Did she dare read something into it?

The emotion glowing in his eyes warmed her heart in
such an unexpected way that she forgot her momentary
concern and pretended, just for a moment, that something
romantic was brewing between them.

She tossed him a playful grin. "I'm glad to hear you
say that, especially when you once thought of me as a
pest."

"Yeah, well, I wish I'd known then who the woman
that little girl was going to grow up to be. Things might
have been…"

His words drifted off, but her heart soared at the

implication. Their gazes locked until he pulled his hand away and muttered, "Dammit."

"What's the matter?" she asked, although she feared what he might say.

"This is a real struggle for me, Sasha."

She had a wild thought that he actually might be attracted to her and waited to hear him out, bracing herself for disappointment.

He merely studied her as if she ought to know just what he was talking about. But she'd be darned if she'd read something nonexistent into it.

Graham raked his fingers through his hair. "I'm feeling things for you that I have no right to feel," he admitted.

"Seriously?"

"I'm afraid so. And I'm sorry, especially since you still belong to another man."

Sasha hadn't "belonged" to anyone in a long time, and if truth be told, the only man she wanted to belong to was Graham.

Don't miss
WED BY FORTUNE
by USA TODAY *bestselling author Judy Duarte,*
available June 2016 wherever
Harlequin® Special Edition books and ebooks are sold.

www.Harlequin.com

Turn your love of reading into
rewards you'll love with

Harlequin My Rewards

**Join for FREE today at
www.HarlequinMyRewards.com**

Earn **FREE BOOKS** of your choice.

Experience **EXCLUSIVE OFFERS** and contests.

Enjoy **BOOK RECOMMENDATIONS**
selected just for you.

PLUS! Sign up now
and get **500** points
right away!

Earn
FREE
REWARDS
HarlequinMyRewards.com
Join
Today!

MYR16R

HARLEQUIN®

A *Romance* FOR EVERY MOOD™

JUST CAN'T GET ENOUGH?

Join our social communities
and talk to us online.

You will have access to the latest
news on upcoming titles and special
promotions, but most importantly,
you can talk to other fans about your
favorite Harlequin reads.

Harlequin.com/Community

Facebook.com/HarlequinBooks

Twitter.com/HarlequinBooks

Pinterest.com/HarlequinBooks

THE WORLD IS BETTER WITH

Romance

Harlequin has everything from contemporary, passionate and heartwarming to suspenseful and inspirational stories.

Whatever your mood,
we have a romance just for you!

Connect with us to find your next great read, special offers and more.

f /HarlequinBooks

🐦 @HarlequinBooks

www.HarlequinBlog.com

www.Harlequin.com/Newsletters

◆ HARLEQUIN®

A *Romance* FOR EVERY MOOD™

www.Harlequin.com